L. RIFKIN

THE NINE LIVES OF Romeo Crumb

LIFE THREE

Stratford Road
Press, Ltd.

This is a work of fiction. Any resemblance to actual persons, living or dead, animals, business, events, or locales is entirely coincidental.

THE NINE LIVES OF ROMEO CRUMB
LIFE THREE

Library of Congress Control Number: 2006928442

ISBN 0-9743221-2-1

Printed in the United States of America.
First Edition

THE NINE LIVES OF RomeoCrumb

Illustrations by Kurt Hartman

LIFE THREE

da
stix

Chapter One

"Alleys, rise up and taste the cowardly stick blood on your paws!" Fidel roared from the depth of his wicked soul. "Be bold! Be confident! Be proud! Romeo and his cowardly friends lay dead in the street! Our hostages are imprisoned upstairs! The Factory is finally ours!"

"Yeah!" the Alleys cheered.

Fidel sat back down and drummed his paw against his leg. Taking in a deep breath, he glared around the rec room from atop his pillow tower. His sinister, red eyes reached the far wall where Bait had sloppily written *Kil da Stix* in mouse blood. Surrounding the room Fidel's exhausted, subservient clan of evil Alleys was sprawled across the tattered pillows and rugs, resting after Romeo's surprise Factory "visit". Writhing in merriment Fidel enjoyed seeing his number one target taunted and chased to his death out a 5-story window. Still high on the nip, Jailbird stuck his clouded head out and confirmed that Romeo, Tabitha, Calvin, and Fluffy were indeed dead. He could see their battered, lifeless bodies on the pavement many stories below. Trying to shake off his drugged state, Jailbird now sat beside his proud leader and quietly cleaned the dust off his paws.

Mr. Shadow's flimsy cage dangled precariously above Fidel's ratty head as he waited for an unlikely chance to escape his certain fate.

"Bait!" Fidel cracked loudly. "Get over here!"

"Right away, boss." Bait said dashing to the impressive throne of pillows.

"Bait, I need you to do something for me. Go outside with Jailbird and drag those Sticks up here!"

Bait stared at Fidel with a blank expression. "Uh, and...dat would be who?"

"Romeo, you fool!" Fidel thundered sending Bait and Jailbird scurrying on their way. "And his pathetic little friends! Bring their bodies to me so I can tie them up before they come back to life." Then Fidel diabolically rubbed his paws together and sinisterly mused, "Won't they be surprised? I'll put them in the..."

"You won't get away with this, Fidel!" Mr. Shadow suddenly yelled from his hanging prison. "You'll pay for this! Pay heavily!"

Fidel slowly turned his head. Mr. Shadow

huddled like a child in the corner of his cardboard cell. "Mr. Shadow," Fidel began as he twiddled the bug jar that dangled from his stolen collar. "Obviously you've forgotten who you are talking to! You are hissing on thin ice, teach!" Callously Fidel flicked a sharp mouse bone in Mr. Shadow's direction piercing him in the head.

Mr. Shadow shivered under his fur, the box rattling as it hung from the frayed ropes.

Moments later Bait, Jailbird, and two other cronies returned to the rec room. They crept to the pillows nervously fumbling with the tassels. Bait's fur was cold, his teeth chattering. Fidel's menacing gang sat coolly at the base of the cushions following the action with their eyes. "Well? Where are they?" Fidel barked. "Where's Romeo's body?"

"We killed da Sticks! We killed da Sticks!" cheered Fink always a few beats behind.

"Shut up, Fink! Where is he, Bait?" Fidel demanded again.

Bait swallowed hard looking up at Fidel. "Well, boss, they...uh..."

"They what, Bait?"

"They wasn't there! Not a one of 'em!" Bait quickly grabbed the nearest cushion and hid under its velvety fabric, biting his lip until it almost bled.

Suddenly Fidel's mountain of pillows began to shake, some of the smaller ones shooting off in different directions. Fidel's body boiled like an egg.

"They aren't there? They aren't there? What do you mean, they aren't there?" He leapt down and viscously yanked Bait in front of him.

"Please don't hurt me!" Bait pleaded. "We looked everywheres! They's gone! Just like dat! Poof!"

"That's impossible!" Fidel snapped. "How could they be gone? Get back out there and find them!"

"But Fidel," Bait cautiously interrupted, "they's really gone! Go see for yourself."

Fidel scowled at Bait and the others, gobs of foam spitting from his mouth. Raising an angry paw out of frustration, he swatted at Mr. Shadow's cardboard prison. The box swayed violently in the air, poor Shadow clawing for dear life at the edges.

In a flash Fidel rushed outside. To his disbelief Bait was right. Romeo and the others were gone. Nowhere to be seen. Fidel stood in the gloom of day and cursed the very ground beneath him.

Down the street empty stores with boarded up windows, abandoned cars, and the occasional 'Going out of Business' sign dotted the bleak landscape. A noose of cold air strangled the city as a sudden and quick volley of hail crashed against the sidewalks and buildings, violent enough to awaken new fears in the people. Times had always been tough for the downtown dwellers, but now it felt like the worst was yet to come. Practically overnight it seemed their city was decaying from within. Mayor Crowman was found dead in his bed, shot two times through the heart. His wife didn't hear a thing. By late evening the news hit the streets. Panic ensued. Nobody went out. Boys and girls stared from their windows at the closed stores and ghostly playgrounds wondering what could have happened. And why?

Near the Factory, a muddy, swift current of old rain water soared along the curb toward the gutter in a hurry to escape the city. In its clutches floated the lifeless little bodies of Romeo, Fluffy, Tabitha, and Calvin. Suctioned to Calvin's head was a blurred reward flyer offering ten dollars for Mr. Sox's safe return. The four dead Sticks slipped into the cement storm drain and disappeared from the outside world.

Rushing down a narrow dark and cold labyrinth, a nasty flow of street rubbish smashed against the four cats and stuck to their wet, bloodied fur like glue. With a thud they landed on a concrete block three stories beneath the street as a continual drip of sewer water paraded around their heads.

With his eyes closed, Romeo felt the all-too-familiar sensation of spinning in circles. In his mind he saw images of whirling colors and haunting shapes. Feeling as though he was in a drug induced dream state, his traveling body tumbled toward a long empty tunnel. Though black and ominous, he could see a tiny light at the far end. In midair Romeo paddled with his paws, drawing himself nearer and nearer to the mysterious glow. As he swam closer toward the unknown, a strange feeling of peacefulness came over him. Suddenly the pinprick of light shot forward completely engulfing his body. A dark figure loomed before him. In his death trance Romeo saw the hazy, black shadow begin to take shape. To his astonishment he recognized it right away. It was his mother. Unlike her last ghostly visit, this time she was crying. Her little furry paws grazed over her face drying the tears. She looked to the ground as if Romeo wasn't even there. Romeo called to her, struggling for the words though nothing came out, not even a peep. Just then, Mrs. Gamble looked up and for one brief moment she stared into her son's eyes. Romeo reached for her, his heart pounding. Then with a frown, his mother shook her head and turned from him. Romeo instantly felt himself being forcefully pulled away from the light and back into the cold darkness. At that second his dead eyes popped open for the first time since hitting the pavement from his 5-story fall. Lying beside him were his deceased friends.

Romeo had just awakened from his second death.

He examined his body. Even though healed, it hurt. It hurt a lot. Everything felt bruised and swollen. There was no blood on his fur anymore, though it was splattered all around him. He could feel it. Smell it. "Mom," his weak voice called out believing she may somehow still be there. But she didn't answer.

Romeo rubbed his heavy, tired eyes. He lay motionless for a moment wondering if he might still be dead, or perhaps somehow trapped between life and death. Stuck. Then his vision slowly came into cat focus. He didn't recognize a thing. High above him way beyond fields of rusty pipes and cement pillars was a small dot of an opening. He must have fallen from way up there. Romeo carefully wiggled his sore body out of the muck and away from the pummeling sewer drip. He slowly turned to look at his dead friends. Calvin and Fluffy's eyes were tightly shut, but Tabitha stared morbidly into space, her limp tongue hanging low. Romeo gagged and gently closed her eyelids with his paw.

Coughing up brown, muddy water was an assurance that he was definitely alive. The others would soon be too. He couldn't immediately remember how they all died, though a familiar rage whipped through his body. *It was that evil Fidel,* he reasoned.

Romeo sat up fast clutching his back and groaning like an old man. Once on all wobbly fours, he took a step toward what seemed to be another far-off dot of light, almost like what he saw in death. A shiver quickly shot up his spine. Intrigued and hoping to see his mother again, Romeo tiptoed toward it leaving his friends behind.

An eerie silence permeated this tomb-like cave except for the drone of dripping water. His paws crunched over layers of dead rodents, rocks, cans, broken glass, and sludge. "Ouch!" he cried, a sharp shard of glass sticking into the pad of his foot. Holding his breath, Romeo reached down and yanked it out.

The closer he crept to the light, the scarier it became. It was situated between two very large sheets of jagged wood almost like a window. He could tell it was a small area perhaps intentionally there, perhaps not. Odd noises came from the opposite side, strange, painful noises. He thought he heard someone moaning and swore he could hear running water, though it sounded thick like syrup. Wanting to run back, Romeo's curiosity pulled him on. He held his breath and stepped closer to the wooden structure but it was too high up for him to see through the crack. He looked around for something to stand on. Everything was so dark and puzzling, and he had no idea what he was touching. Finally Romeo saw a shadow of something sturdy. Slowly he stuck out his paw to grab it. It moved. "Yikes!" he cried flying back, his heart racing. But Romeo did what any curious cat would; he stood up and went for it again. After all, he'd come this far. Suddenly whatever it was squeaked and squirmed and scurried away.

His eyes now adjusted to the darkness, Romeo saw that it was only a skinny rat resting on a rotted orange crate. He felt silly and relieved at the same time and remarkably not hungry at all.

Romeo pushed the crate under the wooden window positioning it just right after suffering two nasty splinters. Carefully climbing on top, his legs wobbled and shook, still woozy from his second death. His front paws reached as high as they could toward the opening pulling the rest of his body along. He clawed higher, barely hanging on, and peered through the crack. To Romeo's shocking surprise he saw a sight he'd never forget.

Several feet below him on the other side of the makeshift window was another world. It was a scary world so deep in the ground under the city that he wondered if he had fallen right into hell. Vile smells and grotesque creatures inhabited this freakish cavern. Huge, moldy and chipped cement boulders lined its sides as a filthy river wove through the center filled with floating remains from the sewer above. The few animals he saw had horrible scowls on their ghastly faces. Some were missing legs or ears, others had too many. One had giant, bulging eyes.

Romeo looked up, up, up to his city hiding somewhere high above him, then glared back down into the squalid pit he stood in. A shiver raced through him for he knew exactly where he had landed. He was staring right into the feared Vent City.

Chapter Two

In survival class and on field trips, Mr. Shadow had always described Vent City as the ultimate danger zone. Though his teacher had never actually seen it for himself, he knew it was a horrible place plagued by unspeakable sadness and misery. In spite of their natural curiosity, even the bravest Sticks never ventured into this forbidden world. Mr. Shadow warned that the creatures of Vent City were ruthless and violent with double the evil capacity of even the worst Alley cat. He was certain they were able to kill with only their breath and could eat you in one grisly bite.

Now Romeo found himself staring into this most feared black grotto. His first thought was to run. That's what Mr. Shadow would expect him to do. But as Romeo stood there perilously peeking over the cut out window, his own unique instincts took control. Though still shivering with fear, he was going in.

Beyond the wooden wall was a steep drop. Romeo took one quick glance at his dead friends then heaved himself up onto the edge of the wood. Wiggling into a seated position, he rested a moment inside the frame as he gathered his thoughts. From there he was able to look down at the menacing metropolis below. Again, he stared at the strange and unusual animals prowling around looking troubled and distressed. Hobbling along was an angry little puppy with only one eye and two legs considerably shorter than the others. It limped and fell, bumping into everything in sight. A small bird fluttered off to Romeo's left. Trying to fly, it squawked with half a beak as it flopped around, its tiny wings too small to get good lift. There were other deformed species of cats and birds and mice too. Romeo flinched at the sight of a giant cockroach two times bigger than himself with vulture-like claws.

Suddenly Romeo began to lose his grip. He teetered for a moment. His paws quickly slipped out from under him sending him tumbling forward. Thinking fast he grabbed onto the ledge with his right front paw as his body draped over the wall. Romeo panicked, swinging his dangling back paws. Directly under him was the murky river covered with a thick layer of revolting trash and sewage. Its

Chapter Two

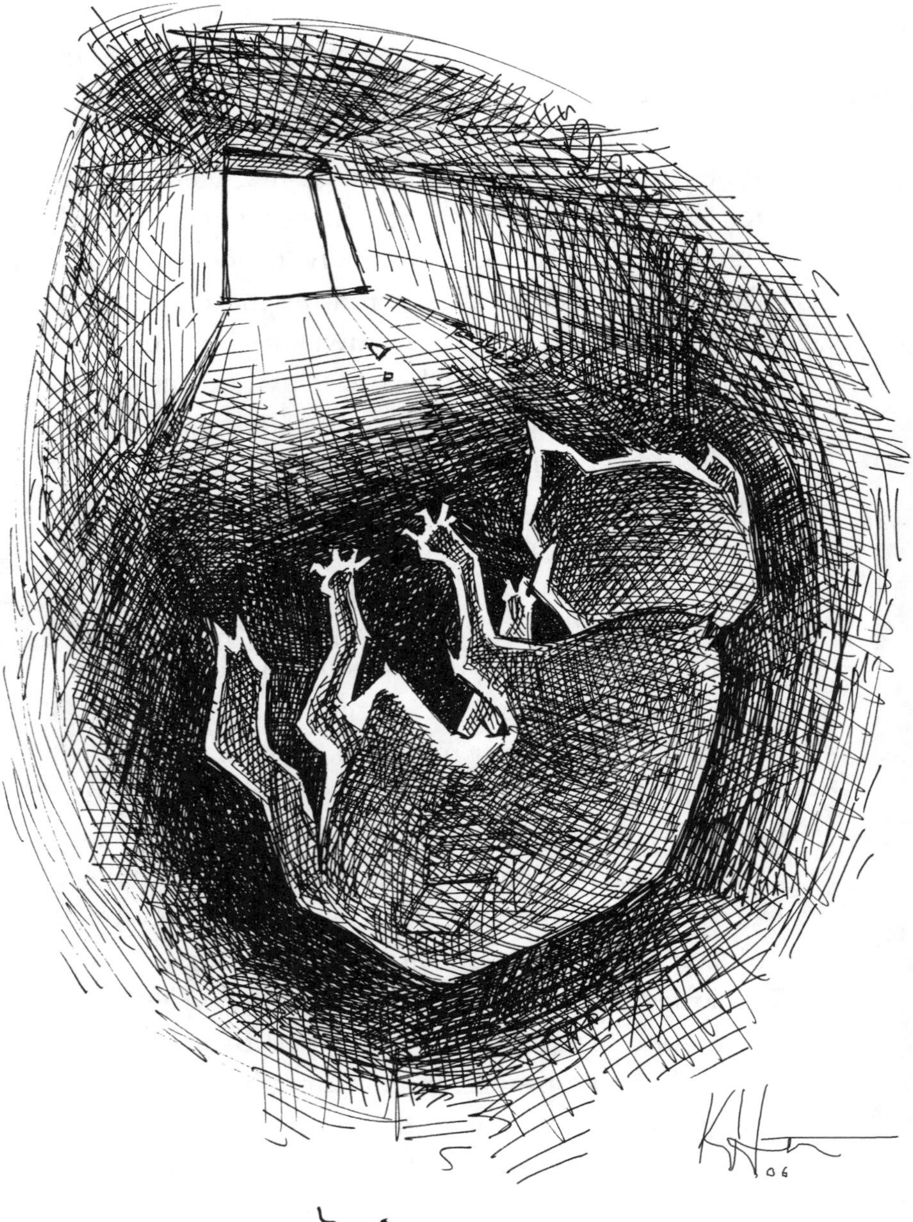

noxious fumes billowed out in hot, steamy clouds. Maybe his bravado wasn't such a good idea. Why hadn't he heeded Mr. Shadow's warning? Still weak from his second death, he struggled to keep himself from falling, but it got harder and harder to hold on. *Get me outta here!* he screamed in his head. *Don't let me die again!* Just then, Romeo felt his paw slip farther and farther down, his claws desperately scraping along the wood. All of a sudden his body was plummeting toward the horrible city below. "Nooooo!!!" he screamed, his voice echoing into the darkness. Flailing his paws violently, he flapped like a bird as if he would somehow fly back up. No such luck. With a thunderous splash, Romeo crashed into the putrid river, mush and goo exploding all around him. He kicked to stay afloat, bits of sewage seeping into his mouth and clogging his eyes and ears. The river's current picked up speed lurching him forward toward the unknown recesses of Vent City. Zooming ahead in the steamy mess, he paddled with all his might barely able to keep from going under. In the near distance Romeo spotted a large pipe jetting out of a wall above the rapid river. It was on the right and approaching fast. If he could only catch it, then he could save himself from drowning in this liquid garbage dump.

As the pipe grew closer and closer, Romeo stretched out his paws as far as he could while paddling his back legs madly. Like body surfing, he smashed up and down distorting and blurring the pipe. Again Romeo reached out his paws to their limit. "One, two, threeee...!" Squinting hard, he thrust himself onto the pipe. It was so slippery he struggled to get a grip. With all the strength in him, he hung on for dear life. All fours were wrapped tightly around the metal as the river below churned on its vengeful wrath. Romeo spit out mouthfuls of yuck and squinted the greasy sludge from his eyes. Suddenly he began to slide back into the river. Screaming and crying, he desperately clung onto the grimy pipe but the tighter he held, the further he sunk. Lower and lower he slipped, bracing himself for the worst, when something grabbed him by the neck. In an instant his body was thrown over the pipe and onto the safety of the ground.

Romeo shook his head not realizing he had been saved. For a second he sat there trying desperately not to breathe in the nasty river smells again. Then it hit him. "Who's out there?" he called, snapping back into the reality of the situation. Rubbing his eyes again, Romeo looked straight ahead at the shadow of a dark figure. Whatever it was had turned the corner and disappeared out of sight.

Though Romeo was anxious to see who saved him, he was more anxious to get out of the sewer and fast. He was feeling nauseous and dizzy. Shaking his fur, Romeo began his search for an immediate escape. His teacher was right. Vent City was no place for him. He turned in all directions. Behind him stood a mountainous heap of broken TVs reaching all the way up to another vent like a crazy ladder. A way out!

Romeo began the adventurous journey up. He scaled the TVs like a mountain climber, making it to the top. After tossing aside a few old newspapers and garbage bags, he reached the metal vent, its spaces large enough for him to slip through. This was easier than he thought. Slithering through the bars, he found himself near the tracks of the 56th Street Subway Station. A rush of relief enveloped his body. Everything was familiar again. That was too close a call! Standing there for a moment, he heard the rumble of the oncoming train. At once his thoughts turned to the strange figure in Vent City who saved him. Why did he do it? What was he? Was he normal? Deformed? And what about Fluffy, Calvin, and Tabitha? Romeo crawled back through the vent into the sewer and stood on the stack of TVs once again. Looking down, he could see the ravenous river sucking its way through the underground. As the train rumbled closer, Romeo wiggled back through the grate and toward the station again.

He now had three choices; hop on a subway car like Mr. Shadow had taught him and head toward the Factory, head home to Dennis, or go back into the sewer for his pals. Certain Calvin, Fluffy, and Tabitha would wake soon from their deaths and climb back out of the vent themselves eliminated that choice quickly. They would probably wonder where he was, but he'd explain his adventure later. His memory of the awful happenings at the Factory made him certain that it wasn't the best place for him right now. Romeo knew Dennis had been missing him for a very, very long time. That was it! He'd go home where he belonged.

Romeo stood at the far wall of the subway tracks glued tightly to the vent's bars. Beneath him throbbed the rolling vibrations of the approaching subway train as dozens of mice scurried to safety into tiny crevices along the tracks. Up ahead on the platform a handful of commuters awaited its arrival, their toes dipping dangerously near the edge.

A fierce wind whipped around Romeo's dirty, smelly body as the subway train stormed into the station. Scrunching his face, he clung firmly to the vent's metal bars. The cracking sound of the subway doors opening echoed through the station as the subway patrons scrambled inside before the warning bell rang. Suddenly the train was off, soaring toward its next destination. The strong subway wind pushed Romeo harder against the vent, coming dangerously close to sucking him into its whirl. After a moment the train and its winds were gone.

Romeo caught his breath and slowly lowered his paws from the bars. Looking down the dark subway tunnel, he brushed the dust from his eyes and pulled the rest of his body off the vent. Knowing the next train would be along at any moment, he quickly dashed across the tracks jumping over soda cans and cigarette butts. He leapt all the way up to the platform. Feeling a little hungry, he was disappointed that the subway mice remained hidden. Then he spotted the exit steps straight ahead. His path was clear now.

Pounding on the cracked, tile platform, Romeo could see the stairs to the street before him. *This was easy,* he said smugly in his head. *I'll be home in no time.* But just as he took a running leap for the fourth step, something struck him in the head. He was suddenly hit again, this time across the back.

"Take that, you blasted varmint!" snapped an elderly man wearing a dirty, old hat. "Get outta my station! Get out! Out!" With his broom, he swung again and again. Romeo ducked and scrambled away from the deranged subway janitor who continued to swat his nasty broom in all directions. Romeo ran in circles, dodging the prickly bristles. Finally he made a beeline through the old man's legs and charged up the staircase like a bull. The janitor held his broom high shouting, "And stay out!"

Romeo hit the sidewalk at record speed. Panting hard, he stopped and leaned against a brick wall, clutching at his chest. As he looked around a scary thought bubbled in his head. He was alone for the first time in a long time in the big, bad city.

Chapter Two

Standing there on the cold street was an awakening moment for Romeo. Emotions he had forgotten about, images he had put aside came rushing back now that he was off the island. Damp, torn flyers of all his friends dangled from lampposts and shop windows, whispering pleas of help. But what could he do? He was still just a kitten. All at once he felt a tangled web of emotions, motivated and inspired, heroic and virile, scared and hopeless. Only two blocks from home, Romeo left his worries on the pavement and dashed away.

Chapter Three

As Romeo raced down the street, the sky grew darker and darker. Night had come and most of the city dwellers were sitting down with their families for dinner, probably discussing the mysterious death of their beloved Mayor. Money was tight for people because of all the strikes, and dinners had gone from hot turkey dumplings to canned soup and beans. Some families didn't even have that. Because of an almost overnight explosion of unemployment, the city was in the early stages of crumbling. The mayor's murder sent a wide spread panic throughout. Afraid a new mayor would impose curfews and raise taxes allowed fears and assumptions to take a big hold of their lives. They unnecessarily started clinging onto every last nickel causing a sharp decline in consumer spending. It was a vicious cycle, and everyone was suffering. If someone didn't come along soon to calm their paranoia, who knew what fate awaited the disheartened citizens.

Romeo felt the cold pavement beneath his paws as he pounded along. He followed the path of sidewalk cracks and holes that had become as familiar to him as any street sign. On his corner he sat under the tall, flickering street lamp and stared up at his building. Romeo had talked to Queen Elizabeth for the first time under that street lamp. It was a special place for him.

Romeo wondered what would happen once he got inside. Would Dennis remember him? Would he welcome him home? Would things be back to normal? Romeo had only been gone a little more than a week, but it seemed like a lifetime. He stepped out of the dusty light and climbed up to his window.

It was open, which was odd on such a chilly night. Romeo instantly knew Dennis had left it that way for him. Feeling tingly inside, he crept under the splintered wooden frame and jumped onto the floor. Dennis wasn't in his room. Lying next to his bed were his favorite muddy shoes. His wallet and toy water gun sat on the desk. Dennis never left the house without them. The cowboy sheets on the bed were exactly as Romeo remembered, messy and all bunched in a ball. Feeling drowsy, Romeo looked forward to sleeping on a comfy bed. He was happy to put the memories of his hard, concrete, island bed in the back of his mind.

Sitting in the middle of the room under a skinny beam of moonlight, Romeo smiled at the bed, the desk, and the pile of laundry. He felt safe for the first time in days. He was home.

Suddenly Romeo heard the sound of Dennis's voice coming from the kitchen. His heart started to thump at the very first syllable. Feeling incredibly excited and nervous, Romeo turned around and darted for the door. This was it, the big reunion. But just as Romeo took his first leap forward, he bumped right into a large plastic bowl of water nearly twice the size of his bowl in the kitchen. That's strange. That wasn't here before, he thought rubbing his sore head. Why would Dennis leave me such a big bowl? I guess he figured I'd be really thirsty when I got home. That Dennis, he's quite a guy. I'm sure a lucky cat. Romeo tapped the bowl with a smile and headed straight for the kitchen.

Romeo slowed down in the hallway listening to the conversation and waiting for the right moment to make his appearance. Then he heard more familiar things. Dennis's mom was laughing, and Dennis had just opened the cookie jar. Romeo recognized the scratchy sound of the chipped porcelain lid. With a wide grin Romeo bounced into the kitchen expecting a joyous welcome. Instead, a shocking surprise awaited him. Dennis was holding what looked like a dog bone, and Mrs. Crumb was filling an even bigger bowl with some sort of mushy stuff. No, it can't be! It can't be! Romeo screamed in his head.

"Romeo!" Dennis hollered. "You're home! You're home! Look, we've got a new puppy!" Little Pierre happily wagged his poofy tail and drooled. Barely bigger than Romeo, he was a white French Poodle with the sweetest, sparkly blue eyes.

Dennis reached down to grab Romeo but it was too late. Romeo was already back in the bedroom shivering uncontrollably under the bed. Following closely behind was Dennis and the puppy. "I can't believe it!" Dennis chimed as he raced through the hall. "He's back! He's back! I knew he'd come back! I knew it!"

Dennis dashed into his room tossing the covers all over the place and laughing like it was Christmas morning. Pierre the puppy immediately picked up Romeo's scent. His black nose poked under the bed skirt and began to sniff feverously. The wet nose under the bed got closer, and soon two glassy eyes glared directly into Romeo's.

"Hisss," Romeo warned, his claws digging into the floor.

"Did you find him, Pierre?"

"Woof! Woof! Woof!" Pierre yelped proudly. Wriggling out, the pooch sat at Dennis's feet.

Dennis knelt down and patted him on his

powder puff head. "Good boy! What a good boy!"

Playfully biting Dennis's hand, the two new buddies fell to the floor rolling around the room. They were having a grand old time playing with Pierre's new squeaky toys, almost as if Dennis had forgotten Romeo was even there. Romeo peeked out of the little space between the floor and the bed skirt and watched his best friend wrestle a dog. He smiled for a moment, always happy to see Dennis smile. However, a creeping loneliness overtook him. What happened Romeo wondered. I was only gone a few days! A dog? How could Dennis get a dog? And such a funny looking one to boot. Seeing Dennis hug Pierre saddened him all the more. That's it, he finally thought. Things will never be the same. The good times are gone forever.

Romeo lowered his head and closed his eyes, when suddenly a hand grabbed him from under the bed. "Come here, silly you," Dennis giggled tickling Romeo's tummy. "Why are you hiding? I knew you'd come home. I just knew it! But hey, what have you gotten into? Look at all this junk in your fur." Dennis brushed Romeo off with his t-shirt and hugged him tight. Pulling Pierre closer, Dennis began the dreaded introductions. "Romeo...Pierre, Pierre...Romeo."

Hesitantly the two animals sat staring each other down. The tension was thick. A cat and a dog in the same room? How could such a thing be?

Just then, Pierre leaned forward frightening

Romeo to the bone. Romeo instantly hissed and arched his back, his hair standing on end. But Pierre didn't bite, he didn't even growl. In fact, he stuck out his long, pink tongue and gave Romeo a friendly lick on the face. Romeo was surprised. He'd learned that dogs were the enemy, but Pierre seemed like a sweet pup. This could possibly work.

"See, you guys are going to be best friends," Dennis beamed. Standing tall, he picked up Romeo and held him high in the air. "I sure missed you, buddy! You had me so scared. Dad thought you got hit by a car and were dead in a ditch where no one could find you." Romeo was showered in kisses, quickly regretting he ever doubted Dennis. He hadn't been forgotten. Things were going to be just great.

Dennis tickled Pierre's ears and pinched his tail. "I'll be right back, you guys. I'm going to get Romeo some food," Dennis said. Romeo smiled. Standing in the doorway Dennis took a quick glance at his two buddies and left for the kitchen.

In the bedroom Romeo and Pierre sat alone for the first time. A little more at ease, Romeo opened his mouth to say hello. As he did, Pierre interrupted in a heavy French accent. "Okay, listen, Monsieur Romeo, zis is my territory now! You just remember zat!"

"But...but," Romeo stuttered, "I thought... what about the...Just a minute now! What was that friendly lick all about?"

Pierre took a big step forward. "Zat was just

for Dennis, no?" he roared. "When he's around, it's going to be real friendly like. But when Dennis is gone," he leaned in very close, "you better watch it, small guy!"

"Huh? I don't understand. I was here first! I'm the territorial one! Where did you come from, anyway?" Romeo asked boldly.

Pierre leaned back against Dennis's toy box and stroked his cotton ball tail. "He thought you were never coming home. His papa got moi from za Pound. I was about to be, how you say, killed, if you can imagine zat. Now zat I'm out of zat dreadful place, I'm going to be Dennis's best friend. As far as I'm concerned, you can just run away again! Bon voyage!"

"I didn't run away, I..."

Just then Dennis burst into the room. "Where are my two little guys?" he called excitedly. "Ah, there you are!"

With Dennis back in the room, Pierre erased his menacing grin and playfully danced around. Each time Dennis turned his back Pierre shot Romeo a nasty glare. Feeling left out and alone, Romeo jumped on the bed and crawled to a warm spot under the covers. "Awe come on, Romeo," Dennis blabbed from the floor, turning Pierre into a canine pretzel. "Come play with us."

Romeo didn't. In fact he stayed under the blanket all night finally nuzzling up to Dennis's knees. Pierre slept on the pillow. "Remember," Pierre whispered late into the night, "my territory now!" Romeo curled himself into a little ball and sank back to sleep.

Later that night Fluffy, Tabitha, and Calvin simultaneously awoke from their deaths drenched in the muck of the sewer. For Fluffy and Tabitha, this was their second death. For Calvin, it was his first.

"It happened again! It happened again!" Fluffy cried. He had never felt so sad. "Oh, why? Why? This is horrible! Only seven more lives to go! At this rate I'll be extinct in no time!"

"Now that was weird," Calvin grumbled, shaking his head back into life. "So that's how it happens. I had no idea how dying felt. To be honest, I never want to go through it again! Never!"

Tabitha wiped the tears from her eyes and sat up straight. "What Calvin? What are you talking about?"

Calvin paced in a circle squinting his eyes and rubbing his head. "It was just like Romeo described, you know, all the swirly shapes and things. Then I was floating down..."

Suddenly Fluffy interrupted, "We know, we know, down a long, dark hallway. It happened to me too. It was real scary until I saw Jack. Who did you see?"

"What do you mean, who? Who's Jack?" Calvin asked, tilting his head to one side.

"Jack, he's my person Cassie's older brother. He died in the hospital of some disease when I just arrived. I guess he really liked me. Anyway, he was there waiting for me, just like the last time. When you die, you see other dead people and animals you know until you come back to life. Didn't you see anyone, Calvin?" Fluffy asked.

"No, I didn't see anyone. Not anyone at all." Calvin's eyes rolled in his head wondering if there was something seriously wrong with him. "Let's say," he finally began, "that I happen to see a pile of bricks at the end of a hall, just hypothetically, of course."

Looking confused, Tabitha crawled over to Fluffy and shared a quick glance. "Well, if you saw bricks, then I guess it must mean something. I don't know what, but it must have some meaning. Don't you think so, Fluffy?"

"Uh, yeah...sure," Fluffy replied with shifty eyes.

"I didn't really see any bricks. I was just making that up," Calvin confessed.

"Then what did you see?" Fluffy probed.

Feeling surprisingly uncomfortable, Calvin quickly changed the subject. "Hey, where are we? And where's Romeo? Wasn't he with us?"

"He's right! Romeo should be here!" Fluffy realized. "Where could he be?" Simultaneously they all shouted for Romeo as loudly as they could. There was no response.

Tabitha quickly looked around the dank sewer. Off in the distance she saw the very same glow that had intrigued Romeo earlier. Little did she or the others know just what lay beyond. "He probably got out," she concluded. "He couldn't wait to get home to Dennis. Come on let's go. This sewer gives me the creeps."

In agreement Fluffy and Calvin looked for an escape without a word to each other. Silently grieving over their own deaths, they trudged through the sludge and slime. After some serious searching, Calvin shouted, "Look! People feet!" Through a grate they could see shoes passing by. The three cats wiggled out of the storm drain and were soon back on the street. One by one they headed home, each in a different direction.

Calvin wondered about those curious bricks that kept popping into his head as he scurried through the dark city streets. Angry and scared, he hurried under the hum of the street lamps trying not to stare at the horrifying reward flyers of all his friends. Romeo, Fluffy, Tabitha, and himself had managed to survive, but did the rest?

Nearing Lloyd's shabby apartment building, Calvin stopped running to catch his breath. Ready to move on, he looked both ways then stepped into the street. All around him were the same signs of the sad, tired city. Suddenly, from out of nowhere a grungy hand with fingerless gloves and dirty nails snatched Calvin tightly around his belly and yanked him high into the air. The scared cat looked down to see a gangly man. His skinny body was layered in old tattered clothes, sewn and re-sewn patches on top of patches. Draped to his muddy boots was a musty, brown coat frayed at the bottom. A floppy, torn hat nearly covered his entire face, but not enough to hide his decayed, yellow teeth. "Well, well, well," he snarled, "if it ain't a little lost pussycat."

Wiggling and squirming Calvin struggled to escape but it was no use. The disgusting man laughed out loud holding Calvin even tighter. His breath was foul smelling. Crumpled in the man's other hand was a ripped piece of paper, a reward flyer Lloyd had taped to the mailbox desperately hoping for the safe return of his beloved cat. On it was a very unflattering photograph of Calvin. Scribbled in black ink under the picture were Calvin's name, Lloyd's name and phone number, and the word REWARD. *Reward,* Calvin thought. He knew Lloyd didn't have much money, and what about that awful photo?

"Lloyd, huh? We'll see just how much Lloyd wants his kitty back, won't we, Calvin?" The stinky catnapper stuffed Calvin under his coat and rounded the corner out of sight.

Back at the Factory Fidel paced around the old rec room bubbling with anger over the loss of

Romeo's body. "He's out there somewhere! We've got to find him! He obviously knows what's going on here, and he's likely to do something about it! I hate those blasted Sticks!"

Bait stumbled into the room, a bugle in his paws. Blowing into the horn, a shrieking, piercing sound echoed throughout the building. Fidel clenched his ears in pain. "Put that darn thing down, Bait! What are you trying to do, deafen us all? Can't you see I'm trying to figure out how to get Romeo and finish him off for good?"

"Uh...sorry boss," Bait said putting the horn behind his back. "Hey, yous can handle that stupid Romeo kid. He'll pop up here sooner or later, then it's curtains. You is da great Fidel."

Fidel grinned proudly at the compliment. "You're right, Bait." Fidel moved closer. "I want that traitor here where I can see his dead body once and for all! Traitors must pay!"

"Oh yeah, I forgot about all that traitor stuff," Bait reminded himself. "But what about all dem other guys? Are you still mad at dem too?"

"All Sticks must pay! Pay for having the nerve to walk through my city!"

Bait threw down his horn and looked around for Jailbird who he now called JB. He was snoring on a shredded rug, bits of nip stuck to his face. Rather than wake him, Bait took pleasure in designing JB's fur into silly styles.

Life Three

Just as he twirled the fur atop Jailbird's head into a sharp point and giggled, Fidel burst onto the rug. "Come close, come close, my friends," he bellowed gathering all the Alleys around him. Jailbird popped out of his slumber at the sound of Fidel's commanding voice. "Make a circle, everyone. Now!"

"What is it, Fidel?" Max called out.

"Yeah, yous got some good news for us?" Cheeseburger asked rubbing his paws together.

Walking in slow circles, Fidel stiffened his upper lip as he eyed each and every one of his eager cronies. "I do have news. I have decided to offer a reward to anyone, anyone who can find Romeo and those dumb friends of his and bring them to me."

"What kind of reward?" Clank wondered. "Will we get to torture 'em?"

Fidel smiled at the word torture. "Bait here will find several plump mice for the winner, to be eaten of course at his leisure. Won't ya, Bait?"

Bait looked around the room. His jaw dropped low and he picked at his whiskers. "But, uh...boss, what if I finds the kid and dem others? Who will get the mice for me? Cause I don't think dat..."

"If...," Fidel exploded, "...if you happen to find Romeo or any other Stick, you will get to keep your job! Is that reward enough? Or should I fire you right now? I'm sure there's an opening at the Pound for a dumbbell like you!"

Chapter Three

Shivering in his fur, Bait groveled, "Oh no, boss, yous da best. Really...yeah, I couldn't ask for a better boss. Don't worry, I'll look for dem brats just like the others. I didn't want no reward anyhow. No way! Workin' for yous is da best reward ever."

"Good! Now, get started everyone! What are you all waiting for? Get out there and find my Sticks!" Fidel hissed sending them all scurrying from the rec room, except for Candle.

Candle sat crying in the corner trying to go unnoticed. A shy, young thing, she cowered alone behind a pile of magazines. She wasn't like the other Alleys. Fidel approached, sending a chill up her spine. "Crying? An Alley crying? Why aren't you out there looking for Romeo too? You don't want to disappoint me, do you?" He knelt down and growled right in her face, his eyes squinting sinisterly.

"Oh no, Fidel," she whimpered. "I'll go. I'll go right now." Hesitantly she stood and scurried for the door dragging her head low to the ground. Fidel always scared her.

"Good! Now don't come back till you've found him! Romeo Crumb is mine!" Fidel returned to his pillow-throne to wait for his most hated rival.

Over the next few days Romeo and Pierre were becoming bitter enemies. For a while Romeo was scared of Pierre's canine ways, but his fear quickly changed to hate and jealousy. They fought constantly for Dennis's affection, Pierre usually winning. They didn't agree on anything and competed over who got the most toys. So far, Romeo had him up by one. But Romeo was growing more and more tired of having a dog around the house, especially a snooty French one. Dennis's room had always been his territory, and he didn't want to share it any longer. Pierre, certain he had become the more important pet, didn't want Romeo around either. Dennis, however, was happier than ever with his two furry friends. As much as Romeo hated the idea, he knew he had to find a way to co-exist with this pesky dog or he might find himself homeless.

Monday morning after Dennis went to school, Romeo confronted Pierre. They met in the bedroom under the desk. "Look, you're a dog and I'm a cat. Technically, I'm supposed to be afraid of you. Well, I'm not. I may not like you, but at least you don't scare me anymore."

"Why, I outta..." Pierre growled clenching his left paw into a tight fist.

"Hear me out, Frenchy." Pacing in front of Pierre, Romeo cleared his throat confidently. "The way I see it, we've got two choices."

"Yeah, either you leave or I throw you out on your butt, oui?" Pierre teased spitting out his rubber cheese wedge squeaky toy, which had once belonged to Romeo.

"No, no, listen, you like Dennis, don't you?"

Chapter Three

"But of course," Pierre answered quickly.

"We both know if I left, he'd be real unhappy, right?" Romeo asked cleverly. "After all, before I came back home he was depressed."

"Whatever, chat." Pierre wriggled into a more comfortable position on the bed. "Look, what are you getting at already? I have some serious sleeping to do."

"I figure we're both here to stay. So, we can either go on being enemies or we can try to be friends. I vote for being friends." Romeo suggested. "All this negative energy is a big waste of time."

Pierre mumbled something to himself in French, then his wiggly little nose twitched. "Friends? Friends? Jamais! C'est impossible! Zat's a good one, Romeo. Ha! Friends!" And with that Pierre jumped off the bed and pranced out of the room laughing. A feline friend was something Pierre definitely did not want.

Angry and confused, Romeo jumped to the windowsill and stared off into the city. He hadn't been out in a few days, not since the accident. Knowing he had to go back to the Factory sooner or later, the time had come to put his Alley fears aside and figure out a way to help his hostage friends. It was a big job but somebody had to do it. Nearly every Stick was being held captive under Fidel's evil thumb. There was no telling what awful things Fidel was doing to them. He wondered if Fluffy, Tabitha, and Calvin ever made it out of the sewer. Maybe they would have an answer to this horrible dilemma. Surely Queen Elizabeth would have known just what to do.

Romeo's eyes wandered over to Gwen's room in the building across the way. Her shades were closed, her room dark. He knew Twinkle Toes, now known as Jailbird, wasn't there anymore. No doubt, inside was a sad little girl wondering how she could have lost her two precious cats in such a short period of time.

Later that afternoon several Alleys returned to the Factory from their Stick search. It had been a long day as they turned over every newspaper and magazine, rummaged through trashcans, looked under mailboxes, and questioned other Alleys. Unfortunately nobody had a clue as to Romeo's whereabouts.

"What do you mean you've found nothing?" Fidel thundered, his faithful pack beside him.

Bait stepped forward into Fidel's menacing shadow. "Nothing today, boss, but I'm sure tomorrow will be better. I just knows it will!"

Fidel snarled and turned to some of the others. "What about the rest of you? Max? Honey? Steak? Fink? Anybody?"

One by one they all shook their heads in shame. Romeo had vanished. Suddenly from above Fidel's head, a loud angry voice rang out. "You'll never find Romeo! You'll never get away with this, Fidel! Never!" It was Mr. Shadow swaying back and forth in his box as it hung from the creaky beam.

"Ah, Mr. Shadow," Fidel chimed looking up to face the old Stick. "Why would you say such a stupid thing? Don't I always get my way? I mean I don't see any happy Sticks around here, do you?"

"One day, Fidel, one day I'll..."

"Shut up, teach!" Just then, Fidel got an idea. It was so brilliant he patted himself on the head. "Of course, of course, why didn't I think of this before?"

"What is it, boss? What did ya think up now?" Bait asked excitedly, but Fidel ignored him.

"Jailbird, climb up to the rafters and join our friend Mr. Shadow in his box. I've got something for you to do." Jailbird, still drugged on the nip, did as he was told and hovered over the box. The others watched in breathless anticipation. Mr. Shadow, trying to be brave, shook nervously in the corner. "Mis-ter Shadow," Fidel began with deliberation, "you know where Romeo lives, don't you?"

Mr. Shadow bit his bottom lip. "I'll never tell! You hear me, never!"

"Very well then, have it your way," Fidel said calmly. "Oh Jailbird, why don't you find Mr. Shadow's broken legs and squeeze them as hard as you can. We'll see if he decides to tell then."

Mr. Shadow went pale under his fur. With evil enjoyment Jailbird grabbed Mr. Shadow's back legs.

Below, the other Alleys cheered and egged him on, jealous that it wasn't them carrying out the ghastly task. With his paws tightly wrapped around Mr. Shadow's injured legs, Jailbird peered deeply into his victim's eyes.

"Jailbird, no!" cried Mr. Shadow as the demented cat moved devilishly closer. "Twinkle Toes, it's me! You're one of us, Twinkle Toes! A Stick! Don't you remember? Please, help me!" Mr. Shadow pleaded to his former student.

All of a sudden Twinkle Toes loosened his grip as a softer, sweeter expression fell across his face. For a second he looked confused. Mr. Shadow stared into his eyes and momentarily saw his old friend. It was the Twinkle Toes he had known. Beneath the heavy layer of catnip and brainwashing, the kind Twinkle was still in there somewhere.

"Do it, Jailbird!" Fidel screamed, becoming increasingly obnoxious.

Suddenly Jailbird snapped back into action, a sinister sneer painted on his face. Once again he took a firm hold of Mr. Shadow's legs and with all his strength squeezed hard sending Mr. Shadow into extreme pain.

"Ouch!!!" Shadow cried knocking Jailbird out of the way.

"More, JB!" Fidel ordered, then he yelled to Mr. Shadow again. "Tell me where Romeo lives! Now!"

Chapter Three

"Never, Fidel! Never!"

Below, Bait and the others laughed and cheered for more of the dramatic torture show.

Fidel stroked his tail. "Very well, Shadow, I guess Jailbird will have to give you a heavier dose of..."

With that, Jailbird twisted Shadow's broken legs until the old cat could stand it no longer.

"No! Stop! Have mercy! I can't stand the pain! I'll tell you! Just make him stop!" Mr. Shadow exploded in agony.

"Jailbird, stop!" Fidel ordered. "Get back down here." Jailbird hopped out of the box and scrambled to the floor. Fidel patted him on the head, a job well done. He then looked up at Mr. Shadow. "Alright, teach... spill your guts! Where does Romeo Crumb live?"

Taking in a deep breath, Mr. Shadow caved. In spite of the intense shame he felt at his cowardice, he reluctantly told Fidel exactly where to find Romeo. Immediately Fidel sent his silent pack of five goons racing to Romeo's building. Bait was put in charge and went along in order to report the ghastly details of the capture to Fidel.

Perched once more on his grand stack of pillows, Fidel picked his teeth with his sharp claw and awaited Romeo's arrival. Octavian the spider, who had been hiding high above the mayhem in the rotted knot of an old wooden beam, glared down at the evil cat with watchful eyes.

Chapter Four

Pierre and Romeo sat scowling at one another from opposite sides of the bedroom. Between them lay a paper plate of leftover chicken pieces they were expected to share. The juicy, baked scent filled the room awakening the tiny saliva ducts in their mouths. Prepared for battle, Pierre growled. Romeo hissed. Digging his claws into the floor, Pierre flaunted his little, poodle teeth, thick mucus oozing between them. Romeo arched his back high into the air, his tail blooming out like a flower.

"That chicken is for me!" Romeo argued. "Dennis even said so!"

"Liar! Dennis always gives me his leftovers! You get the cat food!" Pierre snapped. "Le poulet was meant for me!"

"For me!" Romeo shouted.

Chapter Four

"Me!" Pierre screamed.

"Me!"

"Moi!"

This dispute continued until Pierre unexpectedly leapt forward and savagely jumped onto the plate. With meat stuck to his paws and belly, Pierre barbarically ate the tasty bites as some flew off the plate from the fierce wiggling of his body.

"Hissss!" Romeo pounced, landing right on him. With claws extended, Romeo dug into Pierre, ripping out bunches of his white, curly fur. Struggling on the floor, Pierre swatted at Romeo with one paw, grabbing chicken with the other.

"I'm winning! I'm winning, no?" he blurted, bits of crunchy fat shooting from his teeth into Romeo's face. The chicken was all gone.

Romeo realized he had lost the fight. Hopelessly defeated, he retracted his claws, jumped onto the desk and sighed. Feeling down in the dumps, he sat there watching Pierre devilishly lick his paws clean. Looking out the window Romeo whispered to himself. "I guess this place just isn't big enough for the two of us." Just then, Romeo caught the sad sight of Gwen crying. Her desk was covered in cards and flowers. In her hands she clutched a photograph of a cat.

"Giving up so fast, little kitty-cat?" Pierre teased, tossing the paper plate aside. "I'm not surprised you'd cave so quickly." Leaping onto the bed, Pierre snidely nuzzled himself into Romeo's favorite sleeping spot.

Romeo shot him a stare. "I need to get out of here for a while. I'm going for a walk. Maybe I'll go to Fluffy's. Anyway, I've got some serious thinking to do," Romeo snarled.

"Thinking? Thinking?" Pierre said bewildered. "Who would want to do zat? You cats can be so stupid."

Romeo slipped out the window and carefully climbed down to the street, something he knew Pierre could never do. Aware of the ongoing Alley dangers, Romeo had armed himself with two strong rubber bands he found on Dennis's floor, just like he had been taught in combat class. Romeo quickly walked up and down the safer sidewalks, trying to make sense out of his changing life. He soon found himself standing at the stoop of Fluffy's building. It was time to decide what to do about Fidel and his hold over the Factory. Time to get involved. With determination, he climbed up to Fluffy's window.

Meanwhile, Buggles Flannigan, unsuccessful bank robber, sat in his dingy studio apartment on the eastern edge of the city. He held Calvin up to his face. "You're going to make me rich, Calvin!" he barked with whiskey breath. Shivering with fright, Calvin cried helplessly. After all the trouble and danger he faced getting off the island, only to come home to this. Calvin was beside himself with desperation.

Grabbing the phone, Buggles dialed Lloyd's

number that was printed on the flyer with his dirtiest finger. While it rang, Buggles laughed through the gaps in his teeth and bounced Calvin against the couch. None of his hissing did one bit of good. Buggles was a tough one.

Suddenly, a voice chimed from the other end. "Hello?" Lloyd answered.

Buggles spoke in a deep, low voice. "This Lloyd?" He said Lloyd as if it was the stupidest name he'd ever heard.

"Yeah, this is Lloyd. Who...who is this?" he asked with marked hesitation.

"You want your kitty back?" Buggles teased menacingly.

"Uh, what? Yes? Who is this? Calvin? Are you there, sweetie?"

Dropping the phone, Buggles laughed louder rolling his eyes at Calvin. "He called you sweetie," Buggles teased. "Yeah buddy, I got sweetie here. What's it to ya?"

"What have you done to him? I want Calvin back!" Lloyd whined.

"You want him back, old man?" Buggles growled slowly. "Then how much is his mangy life worth to ya?"

Just then, Buggles grabbed Calvin tightly around the neck, shoved his face up to the phone and pinched his bottom. Calvin roared into the receiver, crying out in pain.

Lloyd listened in horror. "Oh, oh my! Oh my! Calvin? Calvin, are you alright? Speak to me, buddy! Speak to me!"

"Listen, bub, you want your cat or not?" Buggles snapped.

"Of course! Of course I do!"

Buggles dropped Calvin to the floor. "Okay, you'll get him back in one clean piece, see if we can work out a little...deal, see?"

"Well, the flyer clearly says," Lloyd yakked nervously, "that whoever finds Calvin will get a twenty dollar reward..."

"Twenty dollars? Twenty dollars? Do you think I'm stupid? Is that it Lloyd? Because I could just take precious little Calvin here and..."

"No, no! You're not stupid, mister. I'm sure you're a very smart man, very, very smart." Lloyd recovered. "What did you have in mind?"

"Three thousand! That's the deal!"

"What? Three thousand dollars?" Lloyd belted into the phone. "Where am I going to get three thousand dollars? I barely have the twenty! Please! Isn't there something else I can do? I can clean! How about I clean your apartment say, every week?"

"You got forty-eight hours to come up wit' the money. Wednesday night, ten o'clock, outside Stan's Bagel Bonanza. Be there or it's lights out for kitty! And no cops."

"But wait!" Lloyd cried hearing Buggles

hang up on the other end. "Three thousand dollars! Where in the world am I going to find three-thousand dollars?" Lloyd stuck his head far out his window. "Oh, Calvin!" he yelled. "Where can you be?" Crashing to the windowsill, he wept all night long.

Deep in the vast library of the Factory, Mr. Sox and several other captured Sticks lay huddled on the cold, dusty floor. Among them, Waffles and Vittles, who on account of some cocky decision making after escaping the island, stumbled their way right back into Fidel's clutches. Hardly anyone spoke. There was nothing left to say. Every nasty, evil, vengeful thought about Fidel had already been said and re-said. The hope for escape quickly became impossible, the building being so heavily guarded. Hungry and scared, the Sticks felt they had no choice but to wait out their sentence, or so they called it.

Late into the night as the Alleys slept, young Darla had a thought. Without consulting Mr. Sox, she bravely approached the night guard. Younger than her, Steak was in charge of the captured library Sticks from the hours of twelve midnight to six A.M. He kept himself perched in the doorway reacting to every little noise. Two nights ago, he had captured Uncle Fred, not a very difficult thing to do, as Fred bolted right for the door like a drooling and grunting Neanderthal. In his hyper state, Uncle Fred ran headfirst into the doorway, knocking himself out cold. Steak immediately called for back up. Three Alleys dragged the unconscious Stick back to the others, retying him in his original holding ropes. For two whole days Uncle Fred sat wrapped up in string, hobbling as best he could to the untidy litter box. Somehow, Steak, who hardly assisted in this scenario, got all the credit. Fidel was happy with him.

Gently pushing Snicker's chubby paws out of her way, Darla slowly and mysteriously sauntered up to Steak. In the blue moonlight, she eyed him teasingly, rubbing her neck against the dark wood of the doorway. Steak watched her curiously.

"I bet you like steak, don't ya, Steak?" she asked wiggling her hips and batting her eyes.

"Huh?" Steak said stupidly.

Taking two large steps forward, Darla stood face to face with her prison guard. "I know where you can get a really good slab of beef," she teased, tapping him with her long tail.

"I gots plenty to eat around here. Buzz off, lady." Steak shuffled back and scratched his head.

Darla leaned in again. "What'd you eat today that was so good, Steaky?"

"What's it to you?" Steak snapped again, turning away.

"Just curious," Darla said in a sexy tone. "Come on, tell me."

"Oh, alright. Let's see. Us guards shared a baby mouse, and let me think, oh yeah, I had a roach and two spiders," he remembered, licking his chops.

"A baby mouse and a couple of spiders? That's all for a big, strong guy like you? Fidel's feeding you worse than he's feeding us," she said coyly. "Listen, I know a place where the rats are fat and the meat's always cookin'..."

"Go on, go on," Steak drooled quickly losing his cool, his eyes swirling madly at her beguiling ways.

"Buckets full of crunchy cat food, mountains of tuna, tubs of salmon, and best of all, big, juicy steaks!" Darla said hauntingly.

"Where? Where?"

Believing he was under her feminine spell, Darla whispered in his left ear, "Just two blocks away. You're only two blocks away from every edible delicacy you've ever dreamed of."

"R-really?" Steak stuttered, wiping his sweaty brow. "Just two blocks, you say?"

"Just two blocks. And if you let me walk down that teeny-tiny hallway and out that little bitty window, I could bring you back whatever you desire, salmon, tuna, sirloin, you name it."

"Nope! I can't let you do it! I just can't!" His tummy rumbled loudly. "Hot, meaty steaks?"

Darla devilishly nodded her head.

"The kind wit' fat around da edges?" Steak salivated.

"Yes, exactly. Just let me go, and I'll be back

before you can say yummy. You can trust me, honey. I think you're cute."

Just then, something in the way Darla said honey snapped Steak out of his daze. "No way! You're just trying to trick me! You're not goin' nowhere! Get back on the floor where you belong, you stinkin' Stick!" Steak demanded.

With a sudden burst of energy, Darla knocked Steak out of her way, storming forward. She charged head on for the tiny, boarded up window. In a rage, she ripped off the flimsy wood right at the nail and hoisted herself up. Immediately, Steak bolted after her pounding down the quiet hall. He frantically reached for her tail. Too late to make the jump, Steak watched in horror as Darla's brown and gold body slipped through the window out of sight. Stunned, he slumped to the floor and rattled his brain for a solution. He knew he couldn't go out there and capture her himself. But if he told the others, especially Fidel, what would happen? He would be in terrible trouble for sure. How could he let a puny female escape like that? Maybe one of the outside guards got her, he prayed to himself. But then they'll know I let her get away! Fidel will know! Feeling ashamed and frightened, Steak decided to keep his mouth shut. After all, how much harm could one little female Stick do?

At the back of the library hiding in clear view of the window, Waffles smiled with hope.

"You go girl," he whispered to himself.

Chapter Five

Nearing midnight, Romeo tapped against Fluffy's window. The glass was icy cold and covered with frost. Without any ledge he had to cling onto a small pipe pressed up against the bricks while standing on a tree branch. It was a difficult climb but well worth it if it meant seeing his friend.

It was dark inside. Unlike Romeo and Dennis, Fluffy didn't sleep with his person. He spent his nights on the living room couch. Preferring the alone time, Fluffy had his own private blanket and his own private pillow. It wasn't paradise, but he enjoyed it. Tonight Cassie was just glad to have her Fluffy back home safe and sound. She cried and cried the whole time he was gone. To keep her mind busy, she sewed him little dresses and bows out of old scraps of material her mother had leftover from her part time job at the sofa factory.

Romeo tapped on the glass three more times. He waited a few minutes balancing on the limb. No response. Assuming Fluffy was either sound asleep or not home, he began to climb to the street. Halfway down, he looked up and spotted a small, pink nose pressed against the cold windowpane. He hurried back up the tree and cleared the foggy glass with his paw. "Fluffy? Is that you in there?" he called peering inside.

Two little paws slowly lifted open the window. There in the darkness stood Fluffy dressed in his brand new baby blue satin shirt and matching bow. Fluffy stared at Romeo with the biggest grin ever. Romeo immediately jumped inside giving Fluffy a huge hug. He leaned against him so hard, they fell to the floor like rocks, tumbling around, pulling each other's tail, and playing like two best buds should. Out of breath Fluffy jumped onto the couch planting himself against the pillows. "Wow Romeo, I can't believe I haven't seen you since....since we died!" he said with a tiny smile. "We all hoped you got out of that sewer in one piece."

Romeo sat beside him on the couch. "I know, I know. Tell me, how's it feel to be back? I see Cassie is keeping you as fashionable as ever, eh?"

"Awe, cut it out," Fluffy teased socking Romeo in the arm. "Yeah, I know I look stupid in all this girlie stuff, but it makes her happy. Considering what she went through thinking I was lost for good, I don't mind." He tugged at his bow and giggled. "You know, Tabitha won't leave her home at all. She's too scared to come out. I went there this morning, and she told me to leave. I was planning on finding you tomorrow, but luckily here you are today!"

"Awe, she'll be alright," Romeo said. "She's the strongest of all of us. Have you seen Mr. Shadow?"

"No, but I hope he's okay. I'm really worried about those broken legs."

"Me too," Romeo agreed.

"And what about you, Romeo? What actually happened to you that day we all fell out of the Factory window? How's Dennis? Is everything back to normal? I want details."

Romeo moved to the other side of the couch and dropped his head sadly.

"What is it, buddy? What's wrong?" Fluffy asked nervously.

"Dennis got a dog. His name is Pierre and he's..."

"A dog? A dog?" Fluffy interrupted. "How could he do such a thing? Tell me, has it tried to hurt you? Oh no, does he work for Bull? You're not running away, are you?"

"No, he's just a little French poodle. You know, one of those fancy guys with the perfect doo. He doesn't hurt me, he just makes me feel terrible. Pierre told me that *he's* Dennis's best friend now, and

I should just leave." Romeo whined on the verge of tears.

"Hey, come on now. There's no way that's true! That's just his jealousy talking. Nobody could take away what you and Dennis have. Nobody. Especially some little Frenchie."

"He....he....he....said Dennis was happier when I was gone. That he was glad to be rid of me and to finally have the pet he always wanted, a dog like him." Romeo kicked and punched the pillow, sobbing like a little baby.

Fluffy looked down the long, dark hallway. "Listen, buddy, I know you're upset, but keep it down. I don't want Cassie waking up. She's likely to put you in the red tutu she made me."

Romeo surely didn't want that. After forcing a guy like Fluffy to wear those dreadful outfits, the last thing he needed was to be seen in girly clothes. "I'm sorry. I'll be quiet."

Over the next hour, Fluffy and Romeo relived their island adventure; the tall statue, the creepy spiders, the deadly berries, and of course, good ol' Twitch. They missed him the most. What they didn't miss was constantly being at each other's throats. The guilt they felt over their flaring tempers and macho attitudes actually made them laugh a little for the first time. They couldn't believe how they turned on each other when confronted with life and death problems. Now that they were safely away from it all, they decided to put the whole thing behind them forever. It felt good to simply be friends again.

Fluffy let Romeo share his couch. It was obvious Romeo didn't want to go home. Fluffy couldn't be sure, but he had a strong hunch Romeo was holding something back. Something more important. "Is there something else wrong, Romeo? I mean, besides the Euro-dog."

"Well, I have been meaning to tell you..," Romeo began.

Just then, there was tapping on the window. Startled, Fluffy hid under one of the cushions. The big slab of foam bounced up and down from his quivering body. Frozen solid, Romeo's eyes popped out, and he arched his back. They heard the tapping again. This time louder and faster. "Maybe it's just a tree branch," Romeo whispered hesitantly.

"I don't think so. Those branches are too heavy to tap.

Romeo flung himself to the ground as a sudden shadow moved across the window. Then they heard, "Fluffy? Fluffy, are you in there?" It was a female voice, and it sounded familiar.

Fluffy poked his cautious head out from under the cushion and listened. "Fluffy? Are you home?"

"I know that voice!" he said perking up. "I know it. It's..."

"It's Darla!" the voice called. "Fluffy? Are you in there?"

Instantly, Romeo and Fluffy dashed for the window nearly knocking each other over. Romeo rubbed the glass with his paw, thrusting his face against the cold pane. "It is her! It's Darla! It's Darla!"

Together they lifted the heavy window frame and pulled Darla inside. Unfortunately, Romeo lost his balance, tumbling onto her. Then they both flopped onto Fluffy as all three dropped to the floor with a loud thump. Down the long, dark hallway Fluffy could see Cassie's light go on. "Shhh! Behind the couch! Quick!" he warned.

In a flash, Romeo and Darla shot behind the sofa. Fluffy hopped back to his place on the couch and pretended to be asleep. They heard Cassie's doorknob slowly start to turn. Out walked the tired, little girl, clutching an old plush, brown bear whose eyes and ears were somehow missing. Fluffy had chewed off the eyes on one particularly boring afternoon. As for the ears, they were a mystery.

In her fringy, pink slippers and faded, yellow nightgown, Cassie stumbled down the hall rubbing her eyes with the back of her hand. She yawned twice, the second being the longest and most serious of the two. A sudden chill from the open window whipped passed her body bringing Cassie and her bear closer together. The bear liked being close. "Fluffy, are you out here?" she mumbled, half awake, half asleep. Her mutilated, little doll fell to the floor as she shut the window. "There, that's better."

Chapter Five

With her sleepy eyes, Cassie peered around the room for her cat, finally finding him nuzzled up in the corner of the couch. "Oh, there you are, you little stinker." She always called him her little stinker. "Why don't you come to bed with me tonight? Come along now." Bending over Cassie held out her tired arms and shoved them under Fluffy's belly. With a nudge she tried to lift him, though he wouldn't let her. He stuck his claws deeply into the couch cushion and held on tightly.

"Meow!" he screamed. Cassie had him by his back legs, pulling him like taffy. His growing body stretched all the way from the couch to her cold hands. "Meow!" he shouted again, only louder.

Giving up, Cassie flung him back down. "Oh, alright, you little stinker. Stay on the couch. See you in the morning." After a quick search, she reunited with her stuffed bear and headed back to bed.

Always being the dutiful pet, Fluffy didn't like disappointing Cassie, but he knew she was groggy and would be fast asleep in no time. So he waited. After a moment, Cassie's door closed and her light faded. Positive the coast was clear, he stood on his hind legs and leaned against the top of the couch. "Come on out, guys. She's gone."

Hesitantly creeping into the center of the room, Romeo and Darla came out of hiding. Darla was shaking and clutching her lower belly. Something was wrong. "What's the matter, Darla? Are you scared of

Cassie?" Romeo asked.

Darla bit her lip and shook her head no.

"What is it then? Are you sick?" he asked, sounding more tense this time.

"Litteroom! Where's the litteroom?" she exploded. "I've got to go bad!"

Fluffy made a face and pointed her in the right direction. Apparently, her little bladder problem was with her to stay.

She quickly returned and for a moment they sat in a triangle staring at one another. It had literally been a lifetime since they were all together. "I can't believe you're both back! I can't believe it!" Darla squealed, tears in her eyes.

Without more words, the three friends joined in the warmest, most welcomed group hug. Even Romeo and Fluffy were beginning to get a little misty.

"How did you know we were here?" Fluffy asked breaking the mood.

"I didn't. I checked Romeo's place first, but nobody was there."

"*Nobody*?" Romeo wondered, thinking of Pierre.

"Nope. Nobody. Not even your boy, Dennis," she added.

"He must have gone to his Grandma's tonight," Romeo deduced with a sadness in his voice.

"Well anyway, I took a chance that you'd be home, Fluffy. I figured you'd come here after I saw you at the Factory that...that horrible day," Darla said reluctantly.

"Yeah, that day..," Romeo began, remembering their horrible fall out the fifth floor window.

"Tell me about the island! Tell me everything!" Darla insisted, rubbing her eyes dry. "What happened out there? Was it scary and dangerous? I wish I had been with you."

With great flare, Fluffy told Darla the whole story. Acting out how Mr. Shadow fell, breaking his legs, miming how they all learned to fish, and shaking like Twitch used to do. In turn, Darla shared her daring escape from the Factory and how she outsmarted Steak, the gluttonous Alley guard. She confirmed that Twinkle Toes still lived through his drugged-out, evil alter ego, Jailbird, and described life at the Factory under Fidel's iron paw.

"He makes us sit tied up in the library all day and do nothing. We can't play or even talk. We hardly even eat!"

"Gosh, that's awful!" Romeo rubbed his head and bit his claws.

"And that's not all. Mr. Shadow is jailed in his box that hangs from a ceiling beam in the rec room right over Fidel's head. I've heard rumors that they torture him."

After all the gory stories, Darla paused staring deeply into their eyes. "Look, I didn't want to ask, but I just have to. Did you both lose a life that day you fell out of the fifth floor window? Please tell me you didn't!"

Romeo and Fluffy dropped their shoulders. That's all the answer she needed. "Oh, no!" Darla cried. "I'm so sorry! You poor things! Was it painful?"

"Actually," Fluffy said mournfully remembering his experience in the pirate hole. "I lost another life on the island too. It's a long, sad story. I'll tell it to you another time."

Suddenly Romeo blurted out, "I have something to tell you guys, and you're going to think I'm totally crazy!"

"I already think you're crazy," Fluffy teased, socking Romeo in the side.

"No, seriously," Romeo said again.

Darla put her paw against his. "What is it, Romeo? You can tell us anything."

Swallowing hard and long, Romeo began. "Well, the day we fell out of the Factory window and our bodies were washed into the sewer, I..."

"You what?" Fluffy urged.

"I woke up before you and Tabitha and Calvin did. There was a tiny dot of light in the distance, so I followed it."

"Yeah?" Fluffy replied, listening intently.

"Yeah, and well, I sort of happened to wander into Vent City."

"Vent City!" Fluffy gasped.

"Mr. Shadow said to never go there! Ever!"

Darla reminded him. "What were you thinking?"

Romeo paced around them. "I know, I know, but I just wanted to follow the light. Before I knew it, I had fallen into this murky, underground river and..."

"Murky river?" Fluffy said with disgust, imagining all the foul, grimy things that must have been floating around him. "No wonder you smell."

"*Anyway,* I thought I was going to die again, I really did!" Romeo continued, "but then, somebody saved me for no reason at all! None!"

"Really? Did you talk to it? Was it all gross looking like Twitch?" Fluffy asked perching on the edge of his tail.

"No, no, it was nothing like that. In fact, I think it was just an ordinary cat. It walked away without a word. I didn't even see its face. But now I don't know, I feel like I want to go back there and find whoever it was to say thanks."

"Are you crazy? Go back to Vent City? You'll get killed for sure!" Fluffy rolled his eyes and jumped up on the couch.

"He's right, Romeo," Darla agreed. "Vent City is nothing but trouble!"

"Oh yeah? Then why didn't it kill me if it's so dangerous down there?"

Fluffy and Darla simply shrugged their shoulders in puzzlement.

"Just exactly what are you getting at, Romeo?" Fluffy probed.

"I must go back, and I want you guys to come with me!" He stared at his friends' blank faces and continued. "Something's down there. Something good. Maybe, just maybe, something that could help us beat Fidel. Don't you think it's worth a try?"

Fluffy and Darla sat in heavy thought.

"Tomorrow we go," Fluffy whispered quickly. "Tomorrow we go to Vent City. But you better be right, Romeo. I'm trusting you even though I've got a bad feeling about this."

Letting out a collective sigh, the three Sticks stared somberly into space, privately dreading all that was possibly to come.

Chapter Six

Darla and Romeo headed home very late into the night. "I don't know if I can do this, Romeo," Darla blurted out, perfectly framed beneath a glowing street lamp. "I'm awful scared. I don't really want to go into that pit."

Romeo gave her a nod. "Me neither, but like I said, I have to know what's down there. I know it sounds crazy. I can hardly believe I suggested it," he admitted. "Maybe I'm wrong. Oh, I don't know. Now I'm getting confused. I just don't know what to do."

"Well, that's it. I'm not going!" Darla exploded. "I can't do it! I know I said I would, but on second thought, I'm not going to that horrible place! I'm sorry but I can't go down there!" She dashed down the street as Romeo watched her disappear around a corner.

Life Three

Romeo sluggishly walked the rest of the way home with his head low to the ground. He wondered if his hunch about Vent City was just plain stupid. If he wasn't right and something terrible happened to him or Fluffy, he'd never forgive himself. Never. After all, cat after cat had warned of the dangers lurking deep within the underground danger zone. What made him suddenly think they were so wrong just because something plucked him from another certain death? What about the rest of those...creatures? Would they have done the same thing? According to legend, most likely not. Still, as he walked that last lonely block, he remembered his Factory friends and held onto the fantasy that maybe somebody down there, *somebody*, could help them. Now that Darla had backed out, Romeo had his doubts that Fluffy would show either. It was probably for the best anyway. He had put a terrible burden on their friendship. If he wanted to go back to Vent City, he'd have to go alone.

Finally at Dennis's window, Romeo stood beside a potted plant on the small ledge staring through the glass. For the first time the window was closed. On the other side of it, the room was pitch black, the curtains drawn. No sign of the new puppy anywhere. *That darn Pierre!* Romeo yelled in his head. *He knew I was coming home! He did this on purpose!* Romeo began to bang and bang against the glass. The harder he punched, the more it rattled and shook. After a moment he stopped to press his right ear to the cold window and waited.

Still nothing. He pounded again louder and harder.

"Knock it off, down there! Some people are tryin' to sleep 'round here!" shouted the angry tenant from the window of 6B, his fat body bubbling out of his sleeveless undershirt. Romeo rolled his eyes and went back to his knocking.

Across the alley a tiny light went off in Gwen's room. Her shades were closed leaving nothing for Romeo to see. All of a sudden Romeo heard a shuffling noise coming from inside Dennis's room. It was Pierre peeking through the curtains. His small, black nose jetted out between the two panels of material and pressed against the glass leaving a slimy smudge mark. "Who's zat?" he asked quickly and loudly, his paws holding back the curtain.

"It's me! Let me in Pierre!" Romeo insisted. "I'm freezing out here!"

Pierre stuck his whole face out, his eyes shifting back and forth. "Ah, Romeo! Is anybody with you?"

"No, nobody but me. Are you going to let me in, or what?" Romeo demanded.

"Alright! Alright!" Pierre fiddled with the window managing somehow to unlatch the lock and lift it open. Romeo flopped inside leaping onto Dennis's old desk. He brushed the bits of leaves off his tail. Looking around, he spotted Pierre cowering in the corner behind an old deflated basketball.

Romeo walked right up to him. "What are you doing over here?"

"Are...are zey gone?" Pierre whimpered, trembling all over. "Did you close za window?"

"Is who gone? Who are you talking about?" Romeo asked.

Pierre looked over the basketball. "Zey came for you. For you, Romeo. Six of them. Zey were mean, with za long teeth and scary faces!"

"Six what?" Romeo asked hesitantly, inching his way closer to Pierre.

"Cats! Cats! Six *vicious* cats! *Cats*!" The word alone startled Pierre, sending him plunging under the bed. From beneath the springs and metal frame, Romeo could hear his canine teeth chattering up and down.

"Cats! Oh my gosh! It must have been Fidel looking for me!" Romeo shot back over to the window and shut it tight. He was now terrified.

"It was awful! Zey jumped in here and started tearing za room apart. I didn't know what to do!" Pierre shivered.

"Alright. Calm down. Hey, wait a minute!" Suddenly, Romeo bolted up from the ground. "Aren't you supposed to be a *dog*? Why would *you* be afraid of a few cats? Why didn't *you* do something?"

"Please, Romeo! No, no, no! You don't understand! Zey were so mean and scary! Zey said zey'd bite off my ears if I barked. Please! I couldn't do anyzing!" Pierre crashed to the floor sobbing miserably, clutching his precious, little ears.

Chapter Six

Romeo paced about the room. "Pierre? Pierre, listen. Did they say anything? Anything at all?"

"Just that zey wanted you, that's all. I said you weren't here. I even said it real nice. Then zey left. But zey said zey'd be back! Zey'd be back!" Pierre cried, his tail disappearing under his belly.

"But how did Fidel find out where I live?" Romeo howled. "This is horrible!"

"Fidel wasn't here," Pierre remembered. "It was some other guys."

"You know Fidel?" Romeo asked surprised.

"*Bien sur*! I'm a dog, no?" Pierre slowly crept away from the basketball to the center of the room. "Zey used to talk about him at za Pound. You know, the cats and dogs. I never met him, but I'd know him if I saw him. He's the really mean one, *oui*?"

"You got that right." Romeo sat beside Pierre. "Now you know what I'm going through. He wants to kill me! For good! Fidel and those other Alleys are holding all of my friends prisoner in the Factory! I feel like it's the end of the world!" Romeo grabbed one of Dennis's shoes and twisted the sole.

"I don't understand somezing, Romeo," Pierre began. "Why is Fidel after you? Did you do somezing bad to him, or what?"

With a great sigh, Romeo sat against the bed. "No, I never did anything to him. Nothing. To tell the truth, I don't know why he wants to kill me. But I do know this. My parents were Alleys. Mom had six males including me. Fidel had been waiting for us to be born so he could use us in his army." Romeo looked away. "Mom and dad didn't want us males to be Alleys. They wanted us to have a better life than they had. So, they went behind Fidel's back and left us to be captured by the Pound."

"Why? Who would want their babies to go to the Pound? It's a horrible place!" Pierre growled. "Horrible!"

Romeo licked his lips and continued. "I know, but to them anything was better than living under Fidel's rule. At least at the Pound they knew we had a chance of getting adopted as Sticks. Lucky for me, Dennis came along just before..."

"Before what?" Pierre asked wide-eyed.

"This is the really sad part," Romeo sighed with a frown. "To teach my parents a lesson, Fidel had all of my brothers killed by some mangy members of his gang. Every last one of them. Fidel, himself, killed my mom and dad. I was supposed to be dead too, but I was lucky. I had already been adopted by Dennis. When Fidel found out I had escaped, he vowed to finish the job. Ever since he found out I was alive, he's been on a mission to see me dead for good partly because of what my parents did and partly because I am a Stick. And don't forget, he hates all Sticks! All Alleys do! This fight between the Alleys and the Sticks has been going on for more years than I can count!"

"Wow, what a wild story. That's rough. It

doesn't make a lot of sense, but you cats are weird to me anyway," Pierre teased trying to lighten the somber mood.

"Yeah, well...now I'm really depressed. This just gets worse everyday," Romeo frowned. "If I know Fidel, he'll send his guns back here until I'm dead and gone forever."

Just then, an idea flashed in Romeo's mind. "It just might work," he said out loud. Walking in fast circles around the room, his face lit up and his eyes started to swirl in his head.

"What might work? What are you zinking?"

"Well, you're a dog, right?" Romeo simply asked.

"*Oui.*"

"Okay, if you and some of your dog friends were to go to the Factory and scare the Alleys away, then my friends would be free and Fidel would be the one on the run. Whadaya say, pal?"

Pierre's jaw dropped to the floor. "Are you kidding or somezing? *Moi* go to Le Factory? Scare za Alleys away? Who do you think I am, Bull?"

"Look, I know you've got a lot of dog friends. When you go for your walks you meet up with them, don't you?" Romeo asked.

"*Oui,* I guess."

"Well, when the Alleys see a group of dogs, they'll get scared. You can growl and show your fangs and stuff like that. They'll probably even think Bull is around. Wouldn't you?" Romeo asked excitedly.

"I don't know, Romeo. I don't like za sound of zis." Pierre hopped onto the bed and crawled under a blanket.

"Please!" Romeo begged. "You've got to help! This is guaranteed to work! You're a dog, a strong, fierce creature! What cat wouldn't be afraid of you?"

"You! Zat's who!" Pierre turned his head away, his nose high in the air. "You're not scared of me, and neither were zose six Alleys who broke in here!"

"Awe, come on! I was scared of you at first! Remember? You're a scary dog, really you are," Romeo assured him.

"Look Romeo, I don't really like you. In fact, I wish you weren't here at all. And what's in it for me? I don't think I want to get hurt over the likes of you and your kind."

Romeo explained his sneaky idea. How he wanted Pierre and as many dogs as he could find to burst through the Factory door barking and growling like mad. He taught Pierre everything he knew about the Factory, even drawing him a diagram of doorways, windows, and staircases. Surely, the Alleys would clear out in a panic. Of course, Fidel would be plenty angry once the dust settled. With all the Sticks back together, they could surely stand up to him as the great army they had trained at Stick School to be. As a reward to Pierre, Romeo promised him the best spot on the bed and that he could always be the first one to greet

Dennis after school. After some more negotiations, Pierre finally agreed. He would start gathering up his friends the very next day. Confident in this genius plan, Romeo drifted off to sleep dreaming of the Sticks' triumphant return.

Early the next morning, Romeo awoke to the smell of a burning toaster. Seeing the smoke pour into the hallway, he quickly shot over to the kitchen to see what was up. Mr. Crumb was frantically tossing saucers of cold water onto the smoking toast. Wearing a tiny white apron, he hopped all over the kitchen as it quickly became engulfed in the thick smoke. Suddenly, Mrs. Crumb came dashing down the hall just as the smoke alarm sounded. Pierre was still sleeping on Dennis's bed in the best spot, just as Romeo promised.

"What's going on here?" Mrs. Crumb screamed.

"Nothing! Get back in bed! It's all under control!" Mr. Crumb wanted no assistance from his wife. After all, she was sick with the flu, and it was only fair that he cooked her breakfast this one time.

After a few harrowing moments, the fire subsided and the smoke disappeared. The charred, black toast lay on the porcelain plate he found high in the cupboard. Next to her toast were two strawberries and a cold piece of leftover pork. It seems the refrigerator was mildly bare.

Lucky for Romeo, his bowl was full thanks to

good old Dennis. He spent Monday's lunch money on some extra tuna cans. Swallowing a few hearty bites, Romeo said goodbye to Pierre and headed out the window. "I'll check in with you later tonight!" he called.

"Whatever," Pierre mumbled still comfy on the bed. "Ta-ta."

Eight o'clock sharp found Romeo at 56th Street. There he would sneak into the subway station and head straight for the nearest vent. Looking around, he hoped to see Fluffy coming, though he really didn't expect him to show. Romeo understood. As he ran toward the subway stairs, a voice startled him from behind. "Hey, wait for me, Romeo!" He turned to see Fluffy dashing down the street. The two friends hugged hard and long.

"Are you sure you want to do this, Fluffy?" Romeo asked.

"No, but I'm going anyway," Fluffy quipped. "We're pals, right?"

"Right!" Romeo added as they high-fived. "Darla's not coming."

"What?" Fluffy said surprised. "You're kidding!"

"It's alright, Fluffy. She was too scared."

"Females! Well, what do we do once we're inside?" Fluffy asked nervously. Just hearing those word coming out of his mouth made him all the more worried.

Chapter Six

"I don't know for sure, but I'll take you to the mountain of old TVs. We can climb down them right into Vent City."

Fluffy, doubting this entire expedition, shook his head at Romeo and sighed. "Remind me why we're doing this again, Romeo. I mean, can you imagine what Mr. Sox or Mr. Shadow would say right about now? They'd be so angry! On second thought, maybe we should just go home."

"I'm going to do this whether you go or not! The two of us alone can't drive those Alleys out of the Factory, and if Pierre..." Suddenly, Romeo paused.

"Pierre? That little dog? What does he have to do with this?" Fluffy demanded.

Purposely changing the subject, Romeo cracked a phony smile. "Uh, nothing, nothing at all. So long, Fluff. I'm heading into the subway to find the vent."

Fluffy rolled his eyes. "Well, I'm not letting you go down there alone. Come on."

"Okay," Romeo smiled. "Remember the signal if you see trouble, two meows and a hiss. Got it?"

"Got it!" Fluffy huffed.

Romeo had full intentions of telling Fluffy about Pierre's involvement. A decision he would soon regret.

Just as they were about to slip into the station, Darla suddenly appeared out of nowhere. "I made it! I'm here!" she panted, barely catching her breath.

"I knew I could count on you," Romeo smiled. "I knew it!"

"I still don't want to go, but I just couldn't leave you two all alone."

"I'm glad you're here," Fluffy said. "At least I'm not the only one with doubts."

As they discussed their plan and its bleak possibilities, the electronics store front behind them blared the city's news on its three large TV screens tempting customers as they walked by. Darla immediately became captured by the news report. She began walking closer and closer to the window, finally standing nose to the glass.

"What are you doing, Darla?" Fluffy hollered from the corner. "Get over here."

"Is that? Is that who I think it is?" Romeo stuttered, staring at the TVs.

"Yes!" Fluffy shouted. "That's Calvin! On TV! He's a star!"

To their amazement and shock, Calvin's photograph was all over the news. Lloyd was being interviewed in his apartment by a short, skinny reporter with bright, ugly pants. Lloyd's face looked scared and nervous.

"Tell us, Mr. Lloyd," Bob the reporter began, "when was the last time you saw your actor cat?"

Lloyd cleared his throat and stared blankly into the camera. "About two weeks ago. I think."

With microphone in hand, Bob grilled and probed from Lloyd's couch. "Tell us again, what did the madman say to you on the phone?"

Chapter Six

"Um...he told me to bring him three-thousand dollars by tomorrow night, or else! That's when I called the police," Lloyd added.

"Or else what, *Mr. Lloyd*?" Bob asked.

Lloyd leaned into the microphone. "Or else he'd kill Calvin."

"Shocking! Outrageous!" Bob cried. "Tell me, did he say *how* he'd kill the cat? Would he use his hands? A knife? Perhaps he'd throw him out of a window or..."

"Stop it! Stop asking me these questions!" Lloyd screamed. He ran up to the camera shoving Calvin's photo over the lens. "Someone out there please find my precious Calvin!" he screamed.

Romeo, Fluffy, and Darla watched breathless, completely stunned at this unimaginable twist of events.

"I can't believe it! Our poor Calvin! Catnapped!" Darla cried turning away from the TVs.

"And after all he'd been through on that island," Romeo whimpered. "*Incroyable*!"

"Huh?" Fluffy asked.

"Oh, nothing. It's something I heard Pierre say," Romeo explained.

Fluffy leaned up against the street lamp and scratched his head. "It must have happened when we walked home. We all went our separate ways. I should've walked with him all the way to Lloyd's! He was probably still groggy from those poisonous flowers he ate on the island."

"What flowers?" Darla asked.

"Oh, never mind, it's not important now." Fluffy dropped his head low to the ground, his tail bobbing up and down.

Romeo sat beside him. "Why would you have walked him home? He was perfectly capable of walking alone. Besides, this gives us all the more reason to go into that vent and find help. Now, let's move for Calvin and all the Sticks!" Romeo beamed, one paw raised high in the air.

"You're right!" Fluffy realized. "Let's go!"

Together, the three Sticks marched on to their crusade, driven by spirit and enthusiasm. If there was help down there to find, they *would* find it! They had to!

Once inside the bustling subway station, Fluffy immediately spotted the opening to Vent City. As always, it was the main grate on the far wall of the subway tracks. In front of them, a train was just pulling out with dozens of commuters inside. The last car had no one. The people of the city still believed it to be haunted by an angry, young couple searching for a way home. Now with the station empty, it was the perfect time to plunge ahead.

Without any problems, the three Sticks quickly and cautiously opened the vent and dashed inside. Nobody saw them. Nobody at all.

Once on the other side of the vent, they stood

in almost total darkness except for the tiny shreds of light creeping through the holes. Vibrations of another train zooming by lifted the cats off their feet and thrusted them forward, deeper into the blackness.

Romeo quickly led the others to the ladder of TVs he had climbed up before. There, the Sticks stood atop the TV heap peeking down at the foggy metropolis below. "It's so dark," said Darla nervously looking around. Romeo could just about hear the putrid river as it coughed by, his body all a shiver. Around it misty, black clouds swirled in hazy circles like lost ghosts. Painful echoes bounced off the roof of the sewer becoming all the more deep and foreboding as they plummeted back down like deflated balloons. All three Sticks were petrified.

Darla teetered at the edge of the first TV, quivering, teeth chattering. "I...I...can't do it. I can't do it!"

"Then go back, Darla," Romeo suddenly erupted, "while you still can! I'll understand!"

Aghast, Fluffy joined her on the top of the TV. "Is that the river, Romeo?" he pointed. "I think I can hear it."

Romeo bit his lip and nodded his head. "Yeah, that's the one." Suddenly, Romeo felt a weakness in his knees. "Uh, listen guys, maybe you were right. Maybe we shouldn't do this, I mean..."

"Excuse me? Excuse me?" Fluffy snapped in his face. "We came all the way down here and you're going to leave? No!" He leaned against a wooden beam and folded his paws across his chest, his face riddled with disappointment.

Darla ran up to Fluffy pulling at his tail. "Please! Let's go! Let's go home!"

"No, Fluffy's right, I'm going down there," Romeo declared. "I'm sorry, Fluffy. I don't know what came over me. I guess I got scared for a second."

"Look, we don't have time to be scared. Now, let's not stand here all day thinking about it!" Fluffy reaffirmed. "Romeo, you're in charge of this trip. Lead the way!"

Taking small, timid steps, Romeo hopped from TV to TV, climbing further and further down into the treacherous pit below. Not looking back, his two friends followed in his hesitant footsteps coming dangerously close to falling off the unsteady pile of broken TVs several times. The slightest jolt and the makeshift ladder could all come crashing down, flinging them into the very river that nearly killed young Romeo once before. There was no turning back now.

Romeo, Darla, and Fluffy huddled together beside the steaming bubbly river surveying their surroundings like three little lost children. Though he had been down here once before, Romeo was just as scared and apprehensive as the others, maybe even more so. Still, he went on as the brave one, the experienced one, trying not to show his apprehension.

Chapter Six

Vent City certainly lived up to all its hellish expectations. Garbage everywhere, gooey, slimy bricks, jagged, creepy rock walls that seemed endless. The air was heavy and thick, and choking with rancid, rotten smells. Billions of tiny bubbles, oozing and gurgling thick yucky burps of sticky muck burst in the river. Fluffy clenched his tummy, gagging over a rock. Darla held her nose at the putrid water. Whipping his head back and forth, Romeo didn't see any of the odd creatures he had seen before, not the strange bird, the wobbling puppy, or his mystery hero. In fact, the place seemed deserted almost as if nobody was around at all.

"So, where are all the weirdoes?" Fluffy suddenly asked.

Romeo glared at him. "Cut it out! They're out here somewhere! I know it!"

"What if they lurch out at us and throw us in that putrid river? How will we get out?" Darla whined, her eyes filled with fright.

"You don't have to worry about that, Darla. Romeo's hero will save us," Fluffy teased. "Right, Romeo?"

"Quit it, already!" Romeo scolded, socking Fluffy in his side. He looked around deciding which way to go." Why don't we head...that way. It looks less dark. We'll be safer, I think." Together, they set off on their long, spine-tingling journey. They followed a narrow path near the small river. From where they stood, it seemed to go on forever in all directions, never beginning, never ending, lit by an unknown source.

"I can't believe I'm actually walking through Vent City," Darla reminded herself. "I feel like I'm in a nightmare."

"Yeah, well, don't get too used to it, my dear," Fluffy said. "I don't plan on staying here very long." As he marched behind Romeo, his eyes frantically darted about shifting between shadows and eerie noises.

"What if this doesn't work, Romeo? What if there's no one down here who can help us? Then what'll we do?" Darla questioned hysterically.

"Calm down! Hopefully Pierre and his friends are working on their plan right now as we speak..," Romeo blurted out a little too quickly.

Fluffy stopped in his tracks. "What are you talking about, Romeo? Pierre, that stupid French dog? What does *Pierre* have to do with all this?"

"I, uh...," Romeo stumbled. "Let's just keep walking. I think I recognize this part coming up."

"Just hold up a minute. Tell us about Pierre and his plan right now! Obviously something is going on," Fluffy said suspiciously.

"Yeah, Romeo," Darla piped in angrily. "What's up with that dog?"

Knowing he was caught, Romeo turned to the others. "Alright, alright. Promise you won't get mad?"

Fluffy and Darla looked at each other, shrugging

their shoulders and nodding their heads.

"Okay, listen," Romeo went on. " Pierre is a dog, right? Well, I made a deal with him."

"What *kind* of deal?" Fluffy demanded.

"You'll love it," Romeo giggled nervously. "See, Pierre and his dog friends will go into the Factory and scare the Alleys out of there. Good idea, huh?"

"Then what the heck are we doing down here? Are you trying to kill us or something?" Fluffy exploded. "Have you gone mad?"

"Gosh, Romeo!" Darla snapped. "You had to wait until we were down here to tell us about this other sure-fire plan? There's no logical reason why we should be down here at all! I should throw you in that river myself, that's what I should do!"

"Please, please, guys! Really, I was going to tell you, I was," Romeo pleaded, backing away. "But look, I don't know if Pierre's plan is going to work. I don't even really know if he's going to go through with it. After all, can we really trust a dog? Think of it as a back up plan."

"Romeo, sometimes you make me so mad!" Darla growled.

"I'm sorry. I guess I was too obsessed with coming back here to look for help. I know you guys don't understand that, and I know it seems silly but I get these hunches, like building that boat on the island!"

Fluffy thought about the boat and how it was

all Romeo's genius idea in the first place. An idea that worked. An idea that got them all home.

"So, I guess this whole thing was a dumb idea," Romeo concluded. "I'm sorry guys, I should have told you before."

"Look, buddy, I know you meant well. You always do. Nobody could argue with that. Why don't we just forget the whole, stupid thing and get out of this dreadful place." Fluffy paused, looking around at the distasteful sights. "Come on, there's nothing for us here. Let's go home and hope Pierre was successful."

"Good idea, Fluffy. Look, I'm not mad anymore," Darla said tenderly. "I just want to get..."

A sudden startling noise caught everyone's attention.

"Did you hear that?" Fluffy whispered, crouching low to the ground.

Romeo pricked up his ears. "Yes, but..."

"There it is again!" Fluffy cried, hearing another loud bang.

"I here voices!" Darla screamed, grabbing Fluffy's tail and dashing for the TVs. "Let's get outta here!"

"Come on, Romeo!" Fluffy shouted. "Move!"

Romeo pointed to a wall. "I think I hear someone crying over there."

Across the river and a short distance away stood a large, stone wall. Muddy grey, it was sloppily built, almost as if the cement poured down from above, drying as it hit the floor. Standing quite tall, it nearly reached the top of the TV ladder enclosing in a large area of Vent City.

Romeo convinced the others to slowly venture over with him. They quickly found an opening just big enough to fit their three little bodies. Hesitantly, they took turns crawling through.

Once on the other side, they suddenly felt warmer. The thick cement shielded them from the stale, cold air blowing down the river. The large, stone wall met others forming not one, but what seemed to be several rooms. Romeo, Fluffy, and Darla found themselves standing in a cavernous, damp chamber, solid cement walls all around them. It was empty and lit by a tall, lone yellow candle in the corner. "This must be some sort of underground building," Romeo suggested.

"I want to go home!" Darla whined.

"Someone must be here," Fluffy said looking at the burning candle.

Peeking his head through an empty doorway, Romeo could see what appeared to be a long hall. Glimpses of light dotted the passageway suggesting more rooms beyond the various walls. The entire place was much larger than it appeared to be from the river. The crying they had heard echoed louder and seemed to be coming from nearby.

"What are you going to do?" Darla asked Romeo. "I don't like the sound of that."

"I guess we should see who's in there. Maybe someone needs help," he suggested.

Fluffy paced back and forth. "Who cares? What if this is a trick? Have you ever thought of that? A trick to get us in here? What if one of the really scary ones is there, just waiting to pounce on us and take our collars?" He ran and hid behind Darla. "I don't know about you, Romeo, but I'm not in the mood to lose another life!"

"Yeah!" Darla squealed, huddling with Fluffy.

"Nobody wants that," Romeo said. "Now, quit it! You're starting to lose your grip on reality and sound like Calvin did on the island. Since I'm the only one who's been down here before, I'll take the lead. I think we should check it out. Maybe somebody's really hurt in there."

"Who cares," Fluffy mumbled under his breath.

"Romeo, you go first," Darla insisted. "I'm in the middle." She squeezed right between their trembling bodies.

The three Sticks tiptoed closer to the whimpering sounds. They were definitely coming from a tiny room sealed shut by a huge, round boulder. Too big to see around and too heavy to move, it was decided somebody must jump on top of it and look inside.

"You do it, Romeo. You're the leader, right?" Darla reminded him. Fluffy nodded in agreement.

"No, you should do it, Darla," Romeo replied.

"You're the smallest. Whadaya say?"

"What does my size have to do with anything?" she questioned.

"You'll be able to get up there easier and without making much noise, don't you think?" Romeo pleaded with his eyes. Fluffy again nodded back in agreement.

Glaring at them, Darla finally acquiesced. With their front paws, Romeo and Fluffy lifted her up as high as they could. She then grabbed hold of the rock, struggling to cling onto its rounded edges. Once at the top Darla planted herself in a position to look through the little crack. Below, Romeo and Fluffy anxiously bobbed up and down.

"I see somebody! I see somebody!" Darla shrieked.

"Shhhhh!!" Romeo blared. "Don't get us caught!"

"What do you see, Darla," Fluffy whispered. "Who's in there?"

Darla focused her eyes hard. "Looks like a girl. A female cat! I think...I'm not sure, but she kind of looks familiar! Yes! I've seen her before!"

"Who is it? Darla, who is it?" Romeo pleaded, crumbling a small pebble in his paw.

Darla looked harder. "I...I don't know. I can't place her. I think she might be tied up. Poor thing, she looks so lonely in there."

"I'm coming up," Romeo said proudly. "Step

down, Darla, maybe I'll recognize her."

Darla carefully slid back down the rock, shaking her body as she landed.

"Is she deformed?" Fluffy asked. "Does she look like a monster?"

"No, she's not a monster. Nothing like that. Just an ordinary cat like us," Darla described.

Romeo made his way to the top of the big rock with a hoist from his pals and stared into the small room. Unable to see clearly, he wiggled forward almost slipping. He immediately spotted the strange girl crying, her back to him. Like Darla thought, her paws were tied together against the wooden rungs of an old, broken chair. Romeo sighed at the sad sight, wondering how this could be happening to such a little cat. She didn't look like the other creatures of Vent City. No deformities. In fact, she seemed to be quite normal, completely intact. Maybe she had washed down the storm drain like he did, only she couldn't get back up. Romeo stuck his head out farther to get a better look. As he stretched, the rock suddenly shifted and creaked. He held his breath and began to slip. As he did, the girl snapped her little head around at the sound. Her eyes met Romeo's. They stared at each other for several long seconds. In that moment, Romeo was not a bit scared for he knew exactly who she was.

"What happened?" Darla shouted up as quietly as she could.

Chapter Six

"We better get out of here!" Fluffy cried.

Romeo stared at the ground looking confused and bewildered. "I know her," he called back. "That's Candle. She's an Alley."

"An Alley?" Darla shouted. "That does it! Let's get out of here now! I'm scared! Come on!"

"Yeah, let's go back!" Fluffy exploded. "This place sure gives me the willies!"

Romeo held them back with a wave of his paw. "Wait just a minute. She may be an Alley, but she sure doesn't act like one. She's terrified of Fidel, and there isn't anything she wouldn't do to get away from him."

"How do you know?" Fluffy asked.

"I just do, alright? I've seen her out on the streets. She's always sad, really sad."

"Just what are you getting at?" asked Darla.

"I don't think we should go anywhere just yet," Romeo began. "Candle's hurt, and I think we should..."

Suddenly, everyone heard a voice coming from one of the other rooms down the hall.

Frozen, Darla dashed over to Fluffy nuzzling herself in his neck. "Who...who was that?"

"It's probably more Alleys!" Fluffy cried. "Candle's probably just a decoy planted here as a trick! They're going to capture us for sure!"

"Don't be ridiculous, Fluffy," Romeo insisted. "Nobody knows we're even down here. Besides, all the important Alleys are back at the Factory. Let's go and..."

Just then, they heard the voice again only this time it sounded like more than one. Like a group. An angry, loud group.

"I think they're over there," Darla said, pointing to the third room on the left. Hesitantly, she stepped forward and pointed. "Yes, they're in that room. I'm sure of it."

With Romeo taking the lead, they all slowly crept over to the third door, leaving Candle and the mystery surrounding her behind.

"I don't like this," Darla whined hearing the strange voices becoming louder and louder.

"Just stay close and don't make a peep," Romeo whispered in her ear.

Unlike the big rock blocking Candle's room, the third opening actually had a door. Slightly ajar, a golden light glowed from under the bottom. Romeo and the others stood numbly staring at it. Out of nervous curiosity, they listened desperate to know who was speaking and what they were saying. Pressing his ear to the door, Romeo eavesdropped with intense interest.

"What do you hear?" Fluffy whispered gnawing at the end of his tail.

"Shhh," Romeo scolded quietly.

"Mumble..grumble...mumble...get the Alleys out...grumble," said a loud, hearty voice from the other side of the door. "Hmph..Alleys gone."

Romeo jumped back. "Somebody in there is talking about the Alleys. They want them gone!"

"Maybe dogs are in there!" Fluffy feared, shoving Romeo back to the door.

Romeo listened again hearing more muffled words and garbled sentences. "I need to see who's in there," he finally said. "I'm going to open the door just a little more."

"Are you crazy?" Darla snapped, peering around the corner. "What if somebody sees you? We'll all get eaten! Just stay back!"

Romeo tightened his lips together, the sad image of Candle still floated in his mind. "No, I'm just going to peek. Nobody will see me, I promise."

Darla sunk to the ground and prayed to Bubastis. Assuming they would all be dead within minutes, she held tightly to Fluffy for comfort.

"Be careful, buddy," Fluffy said shaking like a leaf. "We'll be right here."

Romeo carefully peered through the crack in the door and pushed it open just a sliver. In the middle of the room he could barely make out a large table fashioned from an old refrigerator box. Sitting around it on rusted, iron chairs and splintered crates were horrible mutants, all creepier than Mr. Shadow had described. The bird with the tiny wings sat on one box, the wobbly dog on another. But those two were the least threatening. All of the animals, at least he thought they were animals, were mutated into horrible, vile creatures. A terrible existence. Their faces seemed like melted plastic. Other creatures had ghastly, grisly teeth and humps protruding from everywhere. One in particular had two grossly large, fleshy bumps sticking straight out of its ears, along with one on each paw. Nearly gagging, Romeo forced himself to see as much as he could. It was a hard thing to do. At the far end of the room stood the silhouette of a strong looking animal. This one seemed to be the leader. It paced back and forth on its hind legs, its front left paw tucked neatly behind its back. In its right paw was a large pointer which waved at a chart and map of the city on the wall behind him. As it stepped out of the shadows, Romeo was stunned. It was a cat, just a plain, ordinary cat. *Maybe he's the one who saved me,* Romeo thought in his mind. *It must be! He's the only normal one in there.*

"Come on! Let's get out of here already!" Darla urged. "You saw what's inside, now let's go!" Romeo didn't respond. "Romeo? Are you listening to me, Romeo?" Scared and confused, Darla lunged forward yanking him by the fur on his neck. Losing her grip, she grabbed onto a blue ribbon attached to Fluffy's tail. Fluffy lurched forward landing on Romeo, pushing him right through the door and into the room. All mutant eyes turned toward the commotion.

"Intruders! Intruders!" a drooling, four-toed bird shouted, flapping onto the table. "Get them!"

Romeo opened his mouth to scream but nothing came out as he struggled to his feet. The creatures roared at them, some zooming straight for their heads. Romeo bolted out of the room as Fluffy frantically yanked Darla off her paws. They shot away as fast as they could, running in sheer terror. Down the maze of mud corridors, out the stone entry, back across the river. They flew for their lives, panting heavily as they soared through their subterranean nightmare.

"Don't look back!" Romeo gasped. "Keep going! Keep going!"

Mid-stride, Romeo suddenly heard a painful meow behind him. Without stopping, he turned his head to see Fluffy writhing on the ground. He had twisted his ankle badly. "Go on without me!" Fluffy shouted. "Save yourselves!" Romeo hesitated. He could see the nasty herd of beasts through the dark, sulfurous clouds as they quickly stormed closer.

Darla kept running at breakneck speed, but Romeo darted back for Fluffy. He reached him just as three monstrous mutants leapt forward viciously landing on them both. Like maniacs, the creatures tore into Romeo and Fluffy's fur, clawing viscously with every ounce of force they had. Struggling to stay alive, Romeo and Fluffy fought as hard as they could, using their rubber bands and remembered battle moves. The pain from Fluffy's ankle seemed gone as he scratched for his very survival. Up ahead, Darla watched the terrifying scene in the grips of the thick, odiferous fog belching from the river.

Suddenly one of the mangled animals opened its mouth and shouted, "Alleys! This'll teach you to spy on us!"

Then out of nowhere, Romeo felt a fierce rumble beneath him. The ground rattled and shook with such force opening a gorge in the center like an earthquake. Spilling out of the crevice charged an angry mob of giant, savage rats bigger than any rats Romeo or his friends had ever seen. The sight of the rodents sent the other mutants scurrying away like chickens. Glowing blood red rat eyes and teeth like knives surrounded the two Sticks. Their huge, ratty bodies inched closer, drool oozing from their mouths. Fearing the worst, Romeo and Fluffy shut their eyes tightly. Instantly, the gargantuan, squealing rats catapulted high into the air, kicked out their bottom legs and landed right on top of Romeo and Fluffy. Nearing certain death, Romeo and Fluffy screamed their lungs out as the rats tore at their feline bodies. Suddenly Romeo felt himself being lifted up and flung high into the air. In a seething mass, the rats caught him with their sharp claws, whipping him around like a rag doll. Then Romeo was brutally flung sideways, landing face down in the dirt. Unable to move, he could hear the rats shrilling and torturing poor Fluffy. And just like that, they were gone.

Romeo was beaten badly, especially his face. His eyes swelled together, his fur soaked in his own blood. He lay there nearly unconscious, *completely* unrecognizable, but somehow still alive. Managing to open an eye slightly, he found himself lying at the paws of the strong leader cat he had seen through the crack in the door. On all fours, he loomed over him, anger raging in his eyes. Darla still helplessly watched at a safe distance in disbelief.

"Throw 'em in with the girl, *Mr. G,*" a hairless squirrel called out, eyes unusually crossed. "Tie them Alleys up real good!"

"I'm not an Alley," Romeo struggled to say, blood gurgling in his mouth.

"Then what are you doing here? You are a liar! *Alley liar*!" the leader roared at the top of his massive lungs. Instantly, he lifted his great paw to slice Romeo across the face. Romeo tried lifting himself up in a last self-defense attempt, coming face to face with the leader's backside. As his vision blurred in and out, Romeo suddenly saw something that astounded him even in his near-death haze. Above the cat's left hind leg, mixed into his dirty grey fur, was the faintest hint of a golden diamond, just like the one Romeo had. Romeo was dumbfounded. Could this be?

"It's you! It's you!" Romeo rambled over and over.

"Who *Alley*?" snapped the cat with the golden diamond, his rage echoing though the city.

"I'm...I'm your brother! I'm your brother!" Romeo screamed.

Chapter Six

"I have no brother! What are you talking about? Are you trying to trick me?" the cat roared.

Romeo pointed to his bottom, licking away some of the blood. "See...diamond... You're my brother!" he cried with his one last gasp. "I knew I'd find one of you alive! I always knew it!"

The leader stopped his rampage, took in a deep, serious breath and sat down. For a moment there was complete silence. No one moved. Then he reached forward taking a good look at Romeo's tag. Glancing over Romeo's hip, he examined the diamond hidden in his wet, matted fur. Then the leader cat stood tall and stern. "I didn't realize it was you under all that mess, Romeo. But...I'm not you're brother."

"You're not?" Romeo managed to say, spitting blood into the air. His disappointment brought him to the brink of tears. "How do you know my name? What about the diamond?" With that the sage, powerful cat took Romeo's head in his paws. Romeo recoiled in trembling fear.

"Romeo, I'm you're father," he whispered, his voice filled with emotion.

Romeo took one good look at him and fainted.

Chapter Seven

A few hours later Romeo awoke in a small, vacant room. Fluffy was laying next to him, sprawled across a ripped, bloody sheet. A plastic bowl of water sat by their side. Romeo opened his puffy eyes to find everything blurry and hazy and swirling around in dizzying circles. "Am I dead?" he mumbled weakly, not knowing if anybody else was in the room. Head pounding and tired, he squinted and reached for Fluffy.

"No, Romeo," a voice suddenly called out, "you're not dead. Neither is your friend. You're just a little hurt."

A little? Romeo thought to himself. *That's a joke.* Every last inch of his body ached and throbbed. He knew then that he hadn't died, for if he had his body would have healed by now. Both he and Fluffy were very much alive for they still bore the remains of a lost fight. Tears and gashes galore. Bunches of ripped out hair. Scraped paw pads. They were a yucky, miserable mess, Romeo having suffered the worst of it.

Slowly the fuzzy image of the leader cat became clearer. He was pacing back and forth. In deep shock, Romeo struggled to make some sense out of everything. It must have been a bad dream. After all, his father was dead, killed by Fidel a long time ago. Or was he? Could this all be a trick? It had to be. Doubting everything he had ever known, Romeo watched the cat as he sat down beside him. "Romeo, we have a lot to talk about. I need to explain many things to you. But now is not the time," he paused. "You need to rest. I'll come back later when you're feeling better and then we'll..."

"What do you mean, *later*?" Romeo shouted on the verge of tears. "You tell me you're my father, my *dead* father, and then you tell me to relax and think about it later? Are you crazy, old cat? You better start explaining now, or I'm going to start wondering who you *really* are and what kind of sick game you're playing!"

"I know it's hard to believe, Romeo, but it's really me. I am your father," he said again with a warmth in his voice. "This diamond we both share, your five other brothers each had one too. Your mother thought it was the sign of greatness," he reminded himself. "I have to tell you something, Romeo. You're not going to like this, but your five brothers...they're all dead. So is your dear mother. We only wanted the best for you...for all of you. I don't know what else to say."

Romeo was speechless. Somehow, some way, it had to be real. He felt it deep in his gut. It was the diamond. "Daddy?" he cried. "Is it *really* you? Could it really be you?"

"Yes, Romeo, it's really me."

All through his short life nothing had been broken so much as Romeo's heart at the loss of his entire family. In spite his many injuries, Romeo leapt forward throwing his bloody paws around his father. They hugged forever, Romeo holding on as tightly as he could, never wanting to let go. For a while they cried, savoring every second of their surprise reunion. After a few heartfelt moments, Romeo finally pulled away. "I've always known about mom and the others. Fidel told me. But father," he said, "I don't understand. I thought *you* were dead too."

"Everyone thought I was dead, even Fidel," Mr. Gamble explained. "When Fidel killed your mother and me, he thought he had taken every life out of us, but Fidel miscalculated. I knew I still had one life left. When I awoke from my eighth death, Fidel was sitting there in *that* Alley, waiting for me to be dead for the ninth and final time. I laid very still, trying hard not to make a sound." Mr. Gamble turned away, rubbing his red, teary eyes. "It was hard to play dead, especially knowing your mother was... was..."

"It's okay, dad," Romeo comforted. "I know. There was nothing else you could do."

"Yes well, after a little while, Fidel eventually left. That's when I must have passed out. Two days went by. When I woke up it was a new day and a new week. I could tell Fidel hadn't come back. He just left our bodies in that Alley all alone. Your mother was beginning to decompose. I didn't want to remember her that way. She was always so beautiful," he sighed. "Anyway, I moved her to a nice, warm box over in the corner and said a few special words. She would have liked that."

"That's was nice," Romeo said softly, his heart swelling inside his chest.

"Then, with every last bit of energy I had, I ran. I ran and ran, looking for you, for all my sons. I knew you kittens had been taken to the Pound. I saw the grey van pick you up. When I got there, it was too late. Horrible hissing and screaming sounds roared from the back. My heart sank. I knew what was happening. Fidel had gotten to my boys." Mr. Gamble lowered his head at the memory. "I won't tell you everything I saw, but your brothers were all gone in less than an hour. All their precious nine lives taken forever. It was awful."

"I'm so sorry, dad," Romeo said. "I just don't

know what to say."

"The only thing that kept me going, the only thing giving me strength to go on, was knowing that one son had gotten away. One son was still alive."

"Me? Was that me?" Romeo asked.

"Yes, it was you. I don't know when exactly, but I noticed you missing. I saw Fidel's gang kill my five sons and somebody else's boy. Poor thing was at the wrong place at the wrong time. Though I felt badly for him, I was at least grateful one of *my* sons was still alive. Still out there. After some research, I learned you lived with Dennis."

"You know Dennis?" Romeo piped in.

"Yes. I know Dennis and Queen Elizabeth. In fact, I know a lot about you. I've been watching you on and off these last months, and I am so proud. I knew you'd find your way off that island. I knew my boy could do it."

"There's something I don't understand," Romeo said, his eyes full of confusion. "If you know me, then why didn't you come to me? If I hadn't fallen into the sewer by accident, would we ever have met? Didn't you care about knowing me in person?"

"Of course, Romeo," he said reassuringly. "Of course. It's *because* I did care for you that I had to go into hiding. I had to stay out of the city as much as possible to save your life. When I do go out, I have to be in disguise and I must be very careful. But I wouldn't have stayed away forever. Sooner or later I would've met you, no matter how dangerous it may have been for me. You're my son."

"I don't understand," Romeo whined. "It doesn't make any sense."

"Remember, Fidel and all the other Alleys think I'm dead."

Just then, Fluffy sat up on the table having heard the whole unbelievable tale from its beginning. His body was badly mangled and bumpy. "Romeo? Are you alright? I can't believe this guy is your father."

Looking over at Fluffy only reassured Romeo he wasn't dreaming. Happy he was alive and still with him, Romeo introduced his father. "Dad, this is my best friend, Fluffy. We've been through a lot together."

"Uh, nice to meet you, Mr. Gamble," Fluffy said awed by the entire situation.

"It's nice to finally meet you, Fluffy," Mr. Gamble replied pleasantly. "You two make a good pair. I'm happy Romeo has found such a true friend."

Romeo and Fluffy looked at each other like two embarrassed little kids, each blushing under their collars.

"Mr. Gamble," Fluffy asked boldly, "what were you getting at before? When you said you were saving Romeo's life? What did you mean by that?"

Mr. Gamble took a long look at the two Sticks and rubbed his tired neck. "Well males, it's an awfully long story, but I think this would certainly be the appropriate time to tell it. It's time you knew."

"Go ahead, father," Romeo said anxiously. "We're all ears."

"Well, it all started several years ago. Carnival, the Alley's first leader, and his sons were dead and gone, and Fidel had just come to power. He was not as smart as his ancestors, and it was hard for him to keep control. For a very brief time the Sticks outnumbered the Alleys, and Fidel felt threatened by this. Yes, he had all the power, just like his ancestors, but it seemed only a matter of time before he'd lose it. The Sticks were becoming organized and independent. Plus, the new dogs around town were causing a serious threat. Fidel had to do something drastic. Are you following me so far?"

"Yes, father, I think so," Romeo said. "Mr. Sox told us all about Carnival and how the Sticks came to be."

Mr. Gamble smiled. "Ah, yes, Mr. Sox. I like knowing you have good teachers. Anyway, the city has always had many power plants and factories. There are more outside the city, but downtown has its share."

"What else is outside the city?" Fluffy asked curiously.

"Let's save that question for another time, Fluffy," Mr. Gamble went on. "Anyway, periodically these places load special trucks with huge barrels of toxic waste."

Chapter Seven

"What's toxic waste?" Romeo asked.

Mr. Gamble moved closer. "Toxic waste is very dangerous. It's trash filled with leftover chemicals and poisons, all mixed into one gloppy mess. If it touches you, you could die instantly, or at least get very sick. Fidel knew of the city's toxic waste disposal program and used it to carry out one of his most evil plans. During this time, many animals, not just cats or dogs, but other kinds of city animals lived and played in what is now Vent City. Back then, it wasn't a dark, creepy place, but welcoming and safe and good for hiding. Many Sticks spent afternoons playing on the rafters or running along the pipes."

"But is smells awful," Romeo piped in.

"It's always smelled down here, that's just something we got used to," Mr. Gamble reaffirmed.

"Did the Alleys ever come down here?" Fluffy asked, wondering how this miserable place could ever have been a playground.

"No, hardly ever. The Alleys liked to stay on the streets where the action was. It was their turf. Remember, the Factory was just for Sticks. Lulu created it that way. Vent City was for *anyone* hiding out from the Alleys, any creature at all. Everyone was afraid of them, even some of the smaller, weaker dogs. One day, the toxic waste truck barreled through the city heading for a special place where all the waste was safely destroyed. Knowing the truck's schedule, Fidel had devilishly arranged for several Alleys to run out into the street at the precise moment the truck turned the corner. The truck driver would lose control and crash, the massive barrels of toxic waste would be dumped all over the city and into the sewers. He planned this little venture right near the largest vent in the city. It's near an Alley at 56th and 11th, where Fidel has lived since."

Fluffy stretched his bruised legs and sat up straight. "Why would he plan such a horrible thing?"

"There is no depth to Fidel's evilness, Fluffy. Who could say why he does what he does. All I know is too much power in the paws of an evil cat is a dangerous thing." Mr. Gamble began pacing around the room. "So, Fidel arranged for this whole disastrous plan to destroy scores of animals in the city. After the truck crashed, several tanks of toxic waste flew out of the back. The tops were sealed, so Fidel, sacrificing some of his own lot, ordered a dozen Alleys to open them up. As they did, the hot waste hit their paws and splashed in their eyes. They ran though the streets screaming and melting into a gooey mess. It was ghastly, but once again Fidel got what he wanted. The waste poured down the vent, crashing into the sewer below, hitting anything and anyone in its path with devastating results. Even the truck driver soared away in a nasty, stream of toxic waste. He later died. In fact, some say his ghost haunts the dreaded faraway four corners of Vent City where the rats live, coming

Chapter Seven

out every year on the anniversary of his death."

"Ghosts? Four corners? Where are those? Why are they scarier?" Fluffy asked, shivering on the table.

"Later. Anyway, the people of the city watched in horror, running for their lives," Mr. Gamble went on. "The fumes alone overcame many people, sending them away in ambulances.

"What happened to all the animals who were playing in the vent?" Romeo asked clenching his stomach.

"Many of them died, but many did not. Those who survived suffered a fate worse than death. The toxic waste deformed them, mutilated them into vulgar, repulsive looking monsters. Scared to come out and face the world again, they remained hidden in the depths of the sewer filled with anger and vengeance. Throughout the years, their offspring have mutated over and over again into the rare, almost ghoulish creatures you see down here today. Nobody ever comes near this place because they're too scared. True, many of the animals down here are dreadful, a threat to anyone. But most just want justice against Fidel and the Alleys who did this to them. They aren't looking to hurt anyone else."

"So they're not dangerous?" Romeo interrupted.

"Not most, except for the rats," he said hesitantly. "Most of the animals down here only hate the Alleys.

That's why we got so mad at you two. We thought you were Alleys coming to harm us further." Romeo's father rubbed his eyes and sat down. "Vent City's population has exploded in numbers. Thousands of creatures live down here now, all mutants in one form or another. All because of Fidel and his quest for power."

"Did Fidel ever come down here himself to see what he had done?" Romeo asked.

"No, he sent his cronies to check things out. Supposedly only one got out alive. The others were ripped apart by the bitter creatures that had to live their lives wallowing in misery and pain. No Alley has ever willingly been down here since, aside from the few who are savagely snatched from time to time."

"How do you know all this, Mr. Gamble? Mr. Sox never told us this story before," Fluffy interrupted.

"Yeah, neither did Mr. Shadow," Romeo added.

"That's because they don't know the whole truth. Nobody aside from those who were here at the time know the real story. Most Sticks and Alleys believe, as they have been taught over the years, that the creatures of Vent City became deformed because of the city's sewage system and living for so long in darkness. Many concluded their missing relatives and friends died during a very bad snowstorm that happened about the same time as the toxic spill. Never has anyone ever been told of the real events, not even your highly learned teachers. Not until now."

"It doesn't make sense, dad. How do *you* know all this. Obviously *you* weren't here when all that toxic stuff happened. *You're* not deformed."

"But I was there," Mr. Gamble admitted. "I saw the whole thing. Many of my good friends died that day. I remember like it was yesterday," he went on, pacing with his head low to the ground. "It was a cold, blizzardy day. You're mother and I were going for a walk. When we first met we used to love meeting in the afternoons and going on long walks though City Park. This particular day, we had been out for lunch together when I suddenly heard a loud ruckus. We were on our way to the park and standing near 56th and 11th to be exact, when I saw Fidel across the street signaling to his gang. I just knew he was up to something bad. I could see the toxic waste truck coming down the street and Fidel staring at it with that evil look on his face. When the truck entered the intersection, Fidel gave some sort of signal. I saw his gang immediately dart into the street. It was then that the truck lost control and all the canisters of poison started falling off the back."

"Wow, dad! What'ya do next?"

"Well, I told your mother to wait for me and ran like lightning over to that truck. I saw some Alleys opening up the tanks and figured out what Fidel was doing. I didn't think I could do much alone, but I fought anyway even though many of them were my friends."

"Oh, yeah," Romeo sighed, remembering his father is and always was an Alley cat.

"I tried desperately to keep those tanks closed. I did manage to keep one sealed, just one, but the rest of the waste ran into the vent and down the sewer just the same. I tried to save the cats and other animals that were underground at the time. Fidel's had it in for me ever since. We never did get along much anyway. He always knew I didn't agree with the Alleys' control over all the city's cats." Mr. Gamble put his head to his paws. "Anyway, when I saw all the injured animals in the street crying out in pain, I shouted as loud as I could into the vent. 'Run for your lives! Get out of there!' I yelled it over and over again, but all I could hear coming from belowground was a lot of screaming. It was too late. From that moment on, I never considered myself an Alley again."

"Wow! So then what happened?" Romeo added spellbound.

"This is the worst part. The damage was already done. Fidel was angry, as angry as I'd ever seen him. How dare I turn against a fellow Alley. He swore he'd someday own my unborn children, claiming I was an unfit Alley parent. My blood was tainted. That's why he got so mad when we sent you males away. He had been patiently waiting for the day when my children were born in order to even the score. Waiting so he could steal you all for himself and raise you in the ways of his Alley criminals. He knew your mother and I would never let you guys join his army. However, we never imagined he'd hunt you down at the Pound after we gave you up. I only thought he'd come after me."

"It's okay, dad. I'm proud of you. You're a brave cat," Romeo boasted.

"Thanks, Romeo, thanks." Mr. Gamble sat down. "So you see, I can't risk being seen with you or anyone else for that matter. Many of the Alleys know my face as well as the diamond on my hip. They'd be outraged if they knew we were still alive. Aside from killing me, they'd eventually come after you. You must be very careful. Once Fidel puts two and two together, he'll know who you really are."

"But he already knows me, dad," Romeo said with worry. "Fidel knows all about me. I thought you said you know all about me too."

"I knew you and Fidel were enemies, like he is with every Stick. He hates all Sticks. I just didn't know he had figured out that you are my son. I'm not surprised. That's not good. Don't ever tell him about me. He must never know I'm alive." Mr. Gamble turned away. "I'm sorry, Romeo. I'm sorry for all this."

"No, dad. I understand now," Romeo

reassured. "It all makes sense. And don't worry, you can count on me."

Tired and overwhelmed, Mr. Gamble stood up to leave knowing Romeo would still have many more questions. What was that meeting he stumbled into all about? Did he know about Candle? What was his mom like? And on and on…

"We haven't finished our discussion," Mr. Gamble finally said, "but you two really need your rest. You both look awful."

Romeo and Fluffy looked down at their beaten bodies. Mr. Gamble was right. They looked almost as bad as the Vent City mutants. Almost.

Mr. Gamble patted his son on the head. "I have some business to attend to. You rest and I'll be back in about an hour. We'll talk some more, and then you have to go home. You two don't want your people worrying, do you?"

They shook their heads in agreement.

"Then it's settled, I'll see you in a bit. Relax and don't worry about my story. There's plenty of time for that later."

Later. There was that word again. Later.

Chapter Eight

After some needed rest, Romeo awoke to find Fluffy nudging him in the head. "Wake up," Fluffy whispered. "Come on! Get up! I can hear everybody talking. Let's go listen."

Romeo groggily sat up. Sure enough, from down the hallway came the sounds of a heated discussion. Intrigued, the two Sticks hopped off the table and crept toward the voices. One stood out the most. Mr. Gamble's. It was now forever ingrained deeply into Romeo's brain. He would always recognize his father's voice, no matter where he was.

Romeo and Fluffy stood only paws away from the meeting place. The heavy, black door was slightly ajar, a sharp sliver of light seeping through the crack creating creepy shadows. Standing there in the darkness of the hallway, they could also hear the muffled sounds of Candle's cries from the far room behind them. Knowing she was all tied up and alone pinched Romeo harder than his swelling headache. When he saw his father again, he'd ask if he knew Candle was even there. After all, maybe those big, ugly rats took her without anybody's knowledge. Surely his father could help. His father.

Fluffy tapped Romeo on the shoulder with a hearty nudge. "Hey, Romeo," he mumbled.

"Ouch! Would you quit it, already?" Romeo scolded nearly falling into the room. "Are you trying to get us in trouble?"

"No, no way. Listen, on second thought maybe we should wait for your dad in the other room. He told us to stay put."

Romeo gave Fluffy a sly grin. "The Fluffy I know wouldn't be such a wimp. Maybe you should go chase after Darla."

"Oh, alright, alright, let's just get this over with," he whispered, rolling his eyes. "But remember, when your father gets mad at us, this was *your* idea."

"As long as I have a father, I don't care what happens. Besides, this wasn't my idea. You're the one who woke me up, remember?" Romeo chided.

"Me? Yeah, well it was your idea to come down to Vent City in the first place!" Fluffy reminded him.

"Oh yeah? Well take this!" Romeo teased,

playfully socking Fluffy in the arm. Fluffy punched back accidentally sending them rolling right into the big room once again shocking everyone.

"Traitors! Traitors!" shouted an angry voice.

"Get them!" yelled another.

"No, no, they're not traitors!" Mr. Gamble said lunging forward. "This is Romeo, my son, and his good friend Fluffy. I think they've suffered enough for one day."

"Sorry, Mr. G."

"Yeah, sorry."

At the back of the room, Romeo and Fluffy lay stiffly on their backs. "Here, let me help you two up," said a blurry someone. "Take my wing."

Romeo squinted his eyes to see the hazy image of a pigeon above him. Right away he could tell this was no ordinary pigeon. Jetting out of its swollen, stubby neck was some sort of gross deformity. Looking like an old, rotted onion, it rested right above the bird's left wing. Suddenly, the 'onion' moved.

"God, that's gross!" Fluffy roared, cowering for cover as the strange protrusion pulsed and quivered. "Get me out of here!"

"It moved again! I saw it!" Romeo yelled back. Squinting his eyes, Romeo took another close and quick look. It was an ugly, raison-shape and just about half the size of its head. Aside from that, a sweaty film covered its grey feathers as it struggled to stay airborne. Fluffy and Romeo immediately jumped to their feet.

"Calm down, males! Calm down!" Mr. Gamble reassured. "He won't hurt you. Just relax."

But Romeo and Fluffy had a hard time doing that. After all, who'd ever seen such a thing? They continued to stare at the strange bird.

"Whadaya looking at?" the pigeon asked.

"N..nothing," Fluffy said nervously. "N.. nothing at all."

"Romeo, Fluffy, meet Bradley," Mr. Gamble introduced. "Bradley is what you might call my main assistant around here," Mr. Gamble went on.

As Fluffy's eyes screeched back into focus and his heart slowed to normal, he took a good, long look at the six other unusual animals in the room. Fluffy knew Vent City was weird, but this was beyond disgusting. He gently nudged Romeo in the shoulder. "Hey, get a load of those guys. Can you believe this place?"

"Unreal!" Romeo affirmed. Like two scared babies, Romeo and Fluffy huddled together, sticking to the back wall like glue.

"Why don't I introduce you to everyone, son," Mr. Gamble suggested. "I see you look a *little* confused. I guess when you're here everyday you can forget how startling all these animals can seem."

Romeo and Fluffy were led to the center of the room and given a comfortable place to sit. "These animals are here for a very important session. When you first *stumbled* in this morning," Mr. Gamble began, "we were engaged in one of our daily meetings. Each animal is here to discuss the future of Vent City. As you can see they are severely deformed, not by choice, but by circumstance. After the toxic waste incident, most of the animals that did survive mutated, or changed. They changed into creatures no one in the real world would want to be around. The result is what you see before you. And that's the whole story."

Mr. Gamble walked back to the farthest end of the table and stood beside what resembled a dog, but could easily have been mistaken for a lumpy heap of mashed potatoes. The dog's flabby skin hung low over its eyes, and you couldn't tell where the head ended and the ears began. Whatever it was lay sluggishly on a small scooter for mobility. Romeo and Fluffy sat up straight to get a better look at this floppy animal. "Meet Chester," Mr. Gamble said, patting Chester on his squishy head. "Before the waste tragedy, Chester was destined to be born a young, healthy pup, but not one of Bull's gang. The poison devoured his mother while she was pregnant with him and his siblings, oddly mutating her pups by melting away their bone tissue. His mother was damaged beyond recognition, and all her pups were born boneless. I guess you could say they were lucky. Only some other boneless animals survived. For some reason, Chester and his family were spared."

Chapter Eight

Romeo and Fluffy's mouths hung open as Mr. Gamble approached a regular squirrel with abnormally huge, bulging, veiny eyes almost as big as its own head. It was sickening at first sight, especially when he blinked. Crusty flakes of eye goo crackled onto the floor, and his eyelids smacked against each other sounding like a sloppy eater. He was introduced as Hayward, a highly deformed rodent. Romeo and Fluffy didn't know whether they should vomit or bolt out of there. "Well, you've met Chester and Hayward. What do you think so far?" Mr. Gamble asked.

Romeo felt a painful knot in his stomach. "Great, dad, but maybe Fluffy and I should go back into the other room. Uh, we're still feeling a little...shaky from our injuries."

"Yeah," said Fluffy, trying to imagine a boneless life.

"Nithe tho meeth you," Chester slobbered and drooled. As he talked, his bottom jaw stayed suctioned to the scooter. His shiny, brown fur lay nicely over his lumpy middle.

Romeo nearly gagged. *I wonder how he goes to the bathroom,* he thought to himself.

To their amazement, Mr. Gamble introduced the next animal. It was a horrifying blend of feline features melted together with what appeared to be roach parts. There were pieces of a roach's exoskeleton jetting out all over a cat body with odd, little antennae and strange, wiry legs. It was ghastly. In fact, it resembled the scraps behind the old Chinese restaurant more than anything living. Absolutely painful to look at, Romeo and Fluffy desperately struggled to hold down their breakfast as Mr. Gamble spoke. "Boys, this young lady is Wanda. She's what we call a Jumble."

"A *Jumble*, Mr. Gamble?" Fluffy asked.

"Yes. Some surviving animals who clung together as the toxic waste splattered over them actually melted together. You see, the whole thing happed so fast and was so chaotic that they literally fused, glued by the waste itself. Over time, the two species melded together into one, retaining features of each animal. Thus, the Jumble was formed. There are different degrees of intensity, depending on how much toxic waste was involved. And not limited to just cats and roaches. Some Jumbles are combinations of cats and birds, dogs and squirrels, even dogs and cats, if you can imagine. It's a hard life for these special creatures. Admit it, even you males can barely look at Wanda."

Sad and uncomfortable, poor Wanda stared at the floor.

"I'm sure she's...very nice, dad. We don't mean any disrespect," Romeo said apologetically.

As if they hadn't seen enough, Romeo and Fluffy came face-to-face with even more hideous creatures, all twisted or bloated in one way or another. George, a former rabbit, was among the lot. Once cute and cuddly, his body was now missing several chunks of its original white fur and no longer had its soft, bunny tail. A sharp stub had taken its place.

"And then we have our cat, Myrna," Mr. Gamble concluded. Though Myrna was introduced as a cat, she looked more like an alien.

Romeo tried his best not to stare, but Myrna was somewhat mesmerizing. Her slick, fleshy body looked as though it had been wrapped a thousand times in long, stringy veins and painted with thick strokes of gooey slime. Perhaps it was her unbelievably twisted face with its sad, sad eyes that finally turned him away. Fluffy fainted as soon as he saw her.

"I know she's a sight, Romeo, but she belongs with us and is deserving of a better life," Mr. Gamble firmly explained. "Nobody here needs to be stared at anymore than you do."

"I'm sorry, Myrna," Romeo said shamefully. "I'll try not to stare." But he knew he couldn't help it.

"You see, fellas," Mr. Gamble continued, "like Myrna, a whopping twenty percent of our animals down here have been exposed to a deadly combination of toxic chemicals and noxious fumes. Somehow, someway, sections of their internal body organs have actually changed places with their external tissues, putting them on the outside rather than the inside. It is a dreadful deformity, one we don't know much about. From what we do know, their life span has been greatly reduced and any chance at normalcy is nil. But they are somehow here and alive."

Just then, Fluffy regained consciousness and quickly sat up. "Ahhh!" he shouted seeing Myrna across the room. "A monster! A monster!" He crashed to the ground once again.

"Well, Romeo, that's almost everybody," Mr. Gamble concluded.

"You mean there are more?" Romeo asked again.

"Of course there are more, many more. Just a few mutants are on my team, but dozens live down here. More strange and bizarre abnormalities live and breathe in this place we call home. Hard to believe life can go on, but it's true! Down here we don't judge anyone by how they look."

Romeo sighed heavily and sat back down. Fluffy was still sprawled on the ground cold and stiff but no longer unconscious, just afraid to get up. Meeting some of the animals didn't help to make Romeo feel any more comfortable with them. Images of the savage behavior and violence Mr. Sox and Mr. Shadow had taught at Stick School were fixed in his mind and haunted him. Seeing his father so accepting of these mutants was somewhat comforting, but to him and Fluffy they would be demons for a while yet. Remembering Twitch and how odd he was at first glance gave Romeo some insight into his own preconceived prejudices.

As long as they were quiet, Romeo and Fluffy

were allowed to stay at the meeting while everyone else got back to the issues at hand.

"I still don't get why your dad is down here," Fluffy whispered into Romeo's ear when he finally could speak again. "And why is he in charge? He's not one of them."

"I don't know," Romeo answered. "I don't get it myself."

"Remember what I said, boys," Mr. Gamble warned. "Stay quiet if you plan on attending this meeting." Turning back to his representatives, he motioned for Bradley to continue with the discussion.

"Let's see, we were talking about the attack before Romeo came in," Bradley said in his high-pitched, squeaky voice. "Mr. G, I do believe it was Myrna's turn to speak." Bradley stared ahead with his usual distant, unemotional expression.

"Very well then. Myrna," Mr. Gamble approached.

Myrna cleared her throat and scratched her squishy tissue. "Thank you, Bradley," she said with some obvious difficulty. "Anyway, as I was saying earlier, the time is drawing near. Saturday marks the five-year anniversary of Operation Toxic Waste! We are four days from victory!"

"Yeah!" everyone cheered at the sound of those long awaited words. Lost in the dust, Romeo and Fluffy looked at each other as Romeo tugged on his father's fur.

"Pop?" Romeo asked sweetly. "What's she talking about? What victory?"

"Not now, Romeo," Mr. Gamble grumbled.

Hayward, with his enormous, bloody eyes, leaned into the center of the table, projecting his gritty, little voice. "Myrna's right, we have worked very hard but still have a lot to do. I think we need more time to prepare. We will only be putting ourselves in jeopardy because we haven't thought things out thoroughly enough. I don't want to be the one to get snatched up by Fidel just because we weren't ready. Count me out!"

"But we *do* have it all figured out," Wanda said through her broken antennae. "We've been planning for nearly five years! We go at midnight, each of us in our pre-determined positions. It's all set."

"No, Wanda, it's not all set. We have no idea what we're doing," Hayward shouted. "We decided yesterday that Plan M wasn't going to work. Now, Plan N or O could possibly work if..."

"Listen, listen, we won't get anywhere if we start doubting ourselves now," Mr. Gamble demanded. "Our strategy is clear, concise, and simple enough for everyone to follow. Hayward, I think you're getting a little nervous because the time for action has finally come. You're worried we won't pull through, isn't that it?"

Daringly, Romeo sat up straight. "Will somebody please tell me what the heck you're all talking about?" he shouted. "We're going crazy over here! And why is Candle locked up? Huh?"

Mr. Gamble took in two deep breaths. "Alright, Romeo," he began, a heavy, dark shadow falling across his face. "You may as well know the entire story." Everybody huffed annoyingly. Romeo and his little friend were quickly becoming a nuisance.

Eagerly Romeo and Fluffy nuzzled into some chairs ready to hear more of Vent City's ongoing saga. Hayward sat back and rolled his gargantuan eyes, spraying the animals around him with yucky, dry chunks of sleep.

Mr. Gamble stood and began pacing around the room. "Romeo, Fluffy, I've already told you how Vent City came about, how Fidel used toxic waste to assure his rise to the top of the power ladder."

"Yes, you told us all about that," Romeo said, his ears standing up straight.

"Well, the five year anniversary of that awful date is this Saturday. It is a very serious day for us down here. We've been waiting a long, long time."

"For what?" Fluffy asked quickly.

"It means we are on our way to revenge!" Bradley erupted. "To victory! To sunlight and people and breadcrumbs! I miss bread crumbs the most."

"Calm down, calm down," Mr. Gamble roared.

"For five long years we've been changing, molding, mutating into the creatures you see right now," Hayward continued. "We were normal animals once. We had families and friends and lives that were savagely taken away! We didn't deserve this! My children don't deserve to look like this!"

"We live this life because of the cruel act of one vicious Alley, and it's time for him to pay for what he's done!" Wanda stormed. "I want to feel the rain on my paws, smell the chilly air and run down the busy city streets again. Sure, I'm ugly to look at, but I'm no monster. I'm good inside. I deserve my life back, don't I? He can't keep us down here any longer!"

"The time has come for us to fight," Mr. Gamble went on. "Romeo, the mutants you see here and the others you have yet to meet are known as the Vent City Divisional Army (VCDA). We have been meeting here for five years now, strategizing and constructing the perfect plan for what we like to call VC-Day! Vent City Day! The day we fight back! Everyone's been working long and hard for this. It's going to be brutal, in fact, we may not all survive, but if we win our independence back, it will be worth it!"

Romeo and Fluffy couldn't believe their ears. Revenge against Fidel? A battle plan five years in the making? On the brink of a major war with their greatest enemy was perhaps the answer they, themselves, had been looking for. The two Sticks listened on.

"But why did you wait five years? Why didn't you fight back right away?" Romeo wondered.

"Good question, Romeo. Good question. You

see, at first, everyone had to heal. The dead had to be removed, the remnants of the toxic waste had to be cleaned, a horrible, lengthy task in itself. After a little while, when the burns and gashes stopped hurting, everyone tried to survive down here, thinking a happy life was possible. But they were wrong. Your mother and I started making frequent visits from the city, bringing food and laughter when we could. The longer I spent down here out of my own guilt over being an Alley, the more I began to understand the pain and anger in their hearts."

"But why?" Romeo asked again.

"You see, I wasn't like other Alleys. I knew I was destined to help," Mr. Gamble explained.

"Mom, too?"

"Yes, Romeo. Your mother helped too. And as angry as everybody was, nobody down here wanted to fight. The animals accepted their fate and moved forward. But as time went on, certain scars didn't heal, anger scars, internal scars that will never go away. Soon children were born bearing the same deformities as their parents and the anger increased and increased until one day we decided to do something. Believe me, we considered non-violent methods like trying to talk to Fidel. I was the link between Vent City and Fidel. We hoped he would let everyone come out and face the world again. But he wouldn't hear of it, especially from me, the one cat he hated most. He resented the fact that I would dare help them. My involvement only fueled the anger Fidel had toward your mother and me. Things got even worse for everybody. Fidel threatened to kill all the sewer animals for good if they tried to surface again and show their ugly faces to the world. For a while, he even had Alley guards stationed at the vents throughout the city. So after some hard thinking, we decided to lay low. Fidel thought we had given in to his wrath, but no. We needed time to gain the proper strength and numbers and brainpower to exact our revenge. Five years was just enough time to prepare, and enough time for Fidel to forget about us.

Without your mother and brothers to comfort me, I moved down here permanently. Shortly after arriving, I was appointed leader of the underground society in charge of this military venture." Mr. Gamble smiled a wicked smile and chuckled. "Won't Fidel be surprised when everyone comes charging back?"

"But Mr. Gamble, why would you *choose* to live here and not on the outside?" Fluffy asked loudly. "I understand your need to help, but do you really have to live down here and be a part of their army?" He turned his head looking around at the depressed conditions.

"I live here for the same reason you don't wander around the city," Mr. Gamble explained. "Safety. Fidel thought I was dead along with the rest of my family. I couldn't risk being seen. If he or any other Alleys spotted me, I'd be dead for sure. I wouldn't be able to help out. And I knew I had a young son out there somewhere. I had to stay alive for him. If fact, I'm even more fired up to fight Fidel knowing he has found you." Mr. Gamble stroked Romeo's head. "I can't let him get you. Not again."

Romeo smiled warmly at his dad. "And Candle? What about Candle?" he asked.

"We catnapped her as part of our plan and because she's the least threatening Alley. When the moment to strike comes, she will be used as a decoy. Even if Fidel doesn't like her, he'll fight for her because she belongs to him."

"Don't hurt her, dad," Romeo pleaded.

"We don't plan to. Anyway, now that you know what we're doing and why, I think it's time for you both to go back home," Mr. Gamble grinned, sitting back down.

"Yeah, get out of here. We've got work to do," Bradley snapped. "You're wasting our time."

"That was totally uncalled for!" Mr. Gamble yelled. "Forgive his rudeness, Romeo, but he is right. You two better get going."

"But dad, I've got a great idea about Fidel!" Romeo cried.

"You can tell me tomorrow, son. You really need to go home now. We have much work to do, and you look dreadful."

"I'll be fine, really! But about Fidel..."

"Tell him tomorrow, Romeo," Fluffy urged,

already heading out the door.

Romeo's face fell. His eyes began to tear up. "But dad, remember I also want you to tell me about mom?"

"Tomorrow, son. We'll talk more tomorrow," Mr. Gamble said firmly.

After all their goodbyes, Romeo and Fluffy headed back to the vent. Mr. Gamble showed them the way and arranged for their return the very next day. "Be careful walking home. Look out for those Alleys and be sure to rest. You've got some serious healing to do."

"Thanks, Mr. Gamble," Fluffy mumbled. "It's been...nice meeting you."

Mr. Gamble nodded and waited for Romeo to say something. Romeo looked down, nervously digging his paw into the ground. "Well, father," he began, "I guess I'll see you tomorrow..."

Suddenly, Mr. Gamble leapt forward, squeezing his son with all the love and tenderness he had held inside. Romeo hugged back hard and once again felt a tear roll down his bruised face. Holding tightly to his father, a sudden thought came to him. "It was you, wasn't it?"

"Me? What are you talking about?" Mr. Gamble asked.

"Yeah, it was you who saved me from the river. You're the one who pulled me out."

"Now get along, Romeo. Dennis must be

worried sick," Mr. Gamble said, quickly changing the subject. But looking at Romeo's face, he couldn't help himself. "Yes, Romeo. It was me. I saved you that day. I couldn't believe you were down here. I didn't want you getting hurt." Seeing his son look at him at that moment with his sweet, innocent eyes made his whole, rotten life seem worthwhile. Mr. Gamble knew that together again, he and Romeo could overcome anything. Nothing was going to stand in their way.

Chapter Nine

Back between the cold walls of the Factory, Fidel sat perched atop his pillow mound sucking the tasty marrow from several old mouse bones. Mr. Shadow hovered between great fear and intense pain as he watched from his box suspended high above. Fidel's silent five lay on the ground casually fanning themselves with old newspapers. It was late Tuesday night as Bait and the others returned from their search.

"What do you mean he wasn't home? Are you sure you went to the right place?" Fidel thundered, grabbing Bait by the skin of his neck. "You are *stupid*, after all!"

Bait dangled in mid-air, choking and coughing and shaking like a leaf. "Yeah boss, the little snot wasn't home."

Chapter Nine

"Are you absolutely sure?" Fidel demanded with evil dripping from his lips.

Bait felt his eyes pop out and his blood stop. "Yeah, boss. Nobody's der. We all checked and waited even, but no Romeo."

Steam spewed from Fidel's nostrils as he threw Bait to the ground. Landing flat on the floor, Bait scurried around as Fidel's angry roar continued. "How could he not be home?" Fidel grumbled, flattening the fur atop his head with the bubbling foam that seeped between his crackling teeth. "Where else would he be? Maybe it's your fault!" he shouted up at Mr. Shadow. "Clink! Mustard! Go teach our teacher a lesson for giving us false directions! Jailbird, you help too!"

"No! No! No, Fidel! I promise, I didn't lie!" Mr. Shadow pleaded, the three Alleys climbing his way. "I gave you the right address! I swear! *Swear*! Please don't let them hurt me again!" Mr. Shadow clutched his two shattered legs as if they were sick children.

"Quit bawling Shadow!" Fidel ordered.

Poor Mr. Shadow's wails and cries got louder as Clink, Mustard, and Jailbird taunted him with their claws. Unable to watch, Octavian curled his eight hairy legs over his head.

"Maybe Romeo's not home 'cause he's ridin' around in a taxi, you know, sight seein," snickered Fish, laughing at his own stupid sense of humor.

"Oh, shut up!" Fidel cracked, smacking him with a pillow.

"Just forget about the little bastard," Max whined. "What do you need him for anyways? We gots the Factory and all these other Sticks."

"I thought at least you'd understand, Max! I want *all* Sticks! Not just some! And I especially want *Romeo*! He thinks he's smarter than me! Nobody's smarter than me! *Nobody*!" Leaping down like a dragon, Fidel landed beside Max. Max ran to the back of the room, hiding underneath a large, torn-up book.

"It's okay, it's okay, Fidel," Max pleaded from behind the binding. "I understand, I understand. We'll get him. Don't worry. You always get what you want."

The mood in the room had gone from tense to complete and utter fright. Fidel was losing his marbles. Nobody wanted to be around him when he was like this. His maniacal obsession over Romeo was sending him spiraling down a hateful path, far more dangerous than his usual vicious self. Everyone wanted rid of Romeo, and all Sticks for that matter, but none so much as Fidel.

"I've had enough of you losers for one day," Fidel announced, standing in the broken down hallway door. "I'm going to meet Raven at Smelly's for a drink."

Fidel stumbled out of the building on four

wobbly legs. Watching with relief, the rest of the Alleys, especially Max, felt the blood rushing back through their arteries. Fidel would be gone for a little while giving them all time to chill. But then he'd be back. He'd definitely be back.

Fidel walked the few windy blocks to the bar. Outside, the dark, frosty air whipped through the empty city streets enjoying the silence that was the night.Consumed by his own haunting thoughts, Fidel trudged through the fog right passed Smelly's, his bug jar necklace glowing like the moon. He pounded on for two whole blocks, step after step, possessed by his hunger for power. It wasn't until Fidel spotted a familiar army statue that he realized he had gone too far. For a moment he stood discombobulated and out of sorts, glaring at the tall, stone soldier. He quickly turned back, grunting all the way to the bar.

Finally reaching Smelly's, Fidel burst in remembering how a cowboy did it in an old movie he once saw. The place was deserted save for a few shiftless Alleys, all drunk as skunks, and Thumbs, the somber, but entertaining saxophonist. A mass of bugs hung around the bar, buzzing and zuzzing over spilled beer puddles and some stale pickles Smelly stole from a cafe trashcan. At the center of the bar under the blazing, red light bulb stood Smelly. He looked fatter than usual, or perhaps he merely had his apron on too tight. In his paw was a dented thimble which he cleaned with the same old dirty rag he always used. He spotted Fidel right away. In fact, he had been expecting him. Everybody knew Fidel couldn't go without alcohol for too long. It just wasn't possible.

"Smelly! Smelly, my man," Fidel slurred, already drooling for his first mug of brew. "Fix me a tall one and make it quick. I gotta date." He looked around for his on again/off again gal.

Quickly pouring the beer, Smelly bit his bottom lip knowing he was soon to be the bearer of some bad news. "Uh, listen Fidel, if you's lookin' for Raven, she had to leave."

"What? What did you say?" Fidel rumbled, snatching his beer from Smelly's paw.

"She said to tell you she had to go to the Glitterbox, work or somethin', and you should hook up with her there."

Fidel slammed down his entire brew in one impressive gulp. Slapping the thimble on the bar, he awaited his next beer. "The Glitterbox? Send one of these rats to go get her! I want her here! Now!"

"Well, uh...gee, Fidel. I don't know, see..."

"On second thought, I'll go myself!" Fidel chugged another beer and stormed out of the bar on a mission. Smelly continued scrubbing his thimbles hard with his old, dirty rag.

Once again Fidel found himself on the streets anxiously pounding through his city. After the brisk walk, he finally reached the Glitterbox, another of his sordid nightlife hangouts. He crawled through the pipe lined with soup can labels and burst into the club with the same fanfare he did at Smelly's. Among the shimmery, purple streamers and gaudy tablecloths were a dozen or so drunken Alleys, all males. The only females in the joint were either parading around on stage, shaming their family names, or carrying trays of stupid-juice to the tipsy patrons. At a far table in the darkest corner sat Raven. Though sometimes neurotic and often clingy, Fidel kept her around. He liked the way she smelled.

Raven sipped a capful of beer alone. Her fur glistened against the dull, dirty walls and was attractively fluffed atop her head. She smiled at Fidel, quickly winking in his direction. Catching her eye, Fidel sauntered over motioning for Betty the waitress to follow him. "Max here?" he asked the girl.

"No, Mr. Fidel," Betty politely said, her eyes filled with sleep. "I thought he was still at the Facility, you know, where you've been staying since you robbed it from the Sticks."

"That's *Factory,* you idiot! Factory! Now get me a beer! And step on it!"

Raven sat up straight in her chair, giving Fidel the illusion she had a flatter tummy than she actually did. "Boy, Fidel, you're awfully punchy tonight. Is something wrong?"

"Wrong? Wrong?" Fidel exploded. Quickly recognizing his loss of coolness, he breathed in deeply

Life Three

simmering like a snake. "I'm sorry, Raven, my dear. I haven't even said hello." He wrapped his paw around her.

"Well, hello," Raven said, recognizing Fidel's phony but irresistible charm.

"And how's your day been? Huh?" Fidel asked snottily.

"Oh, fine I guess. I forgot I gotta work tonight. I hoped you'd find me here," she said with a hint of a smile.

"And what time do you get off?" Fidel asked with questionable motives.

"In about an hour. Why?" she teased.

"You know why," he taunted.

Fidel looked around the seedy club for his waitress. "Where's my beer?" he shouted, standing for the whole place to see.

Everything came to a halt as it so often did when Fidel was around. He liked it that way. Betty scurried out from the back with a tray full of beer like a scared little mouse. She nervously spilled three on the floor, finally serving Fidel his drink.

"No tip for you!" Fidel roared. "Now beat it!"

Betty dashed away, eyes full of tears.

Turning to Raven, Fidel moved his chair closer. "Now that we're alone, my pet," he tickled in her furry ear, "whadaya say we split and..."

Suddenly, a loud ruckus boomed from the entrance. It was Bait. Covered in sweat and dirty rain, he zigzagged around the room like a mouse caught in a maze. The whole club watched mystified as Bait wove between the tables in a frenzy, knocking over waitresses, drinks, and breathing like an angry jaguar. "Help! Help!" he started screaming. "Fidel? Where are you? Where are you?"

Fidel raced forward with alarm, slapping Bait out of his hysterics. "What is it? What is it, Bait?" he demanded, clutching him by the ears.

"The dogs! They're attacking the Factory! Come quick! Hurry!"

Fidel zoomed for the door, slipped through the rusted pipe, and sprinted back toward the Factory leaving Raven behind. Bait stumbled behind as always.

Fidel flew block after block, puddle after puddle, splash after splash. After everything he had gained, before everything he had yet to do, he wasn't about to give it all up to a few scraggly dogs. Fidel owned the city. Like it or not, he was intent on keeping it that way.

Fidel charged through the crumbling Factory door, bursting his way into the rec room. At first he saw pillows everywhere, blue ones, red ones, velvet ones. His mountain had been torn apart and scattered all over. Expecting loud howls and an electrifying commotion, he suddenly found himself in the midst of one of the most pathetic examples of animal rank he had ever seen. Standing in a wide circle around the room were Max, Mustard, Steak, Cheeseburger, and several other Alleys. They had angry scowls and heaving chests. In the center of this circle were five dogs, not Bull and his vicious crowd of mongrels, but five little pups, three young Cocker Spaniels, a Beagle, and a French Poodle, poofs and all. They whimpered and shook, glued tightly to one another. One dog in particular whined the loudest. It was Pierre, Dennis's poodle. Fidel walked around the circle looking proudly at his surrounding army. He stared down the five pups. His evil smirk caught Pierre's attention sending him into a deeper panic. Slowly, Fidel leaned forward, his ugly head hovering over the dogs. "Well, well well! What do we have here? Five little puppy dogs. Aw, ain't this sweet," he teased with razor sharp sarcasm.

"Dey tried to fight us, Fidel," Cheeseburger shouted, reaching his toe high into his nose.

"Can you imagine these guys fightin' us?" Max snickered.

Just then, Bait flew into the room clutching his chest and deeply out of breath. "Is everyone dead? Are they still here, boss?" he quivered, covering his eyes with his soggy paw.

"Oh, get over here, Bait," snapped Fidel. "Nobody's dead, *yet*." Glaring at the dogs, he let out a most vile sounding hiss while crouching low and jetting out his claws just to be mean. The puppies continued to shiver, one of them peeing right on Pierre.

"What were you guys thinking coming in here, huh?" Fidel roared.

They all looked down, humiliated. Defeated by cats.

"You may be dogs, but do you think you alone could stop us? Not yet, my little friends," Fidel said laughing in their faces. "Now get outta here before I get really mad! Consider your freedom a warning this time. Next time it's curtains!"

Like a tornado, the five puppies whirled out of there, never looking back or doubting their salvation. Fidel was right. They were in over their heads. Sure they were dogs, technically, but a few tiny, pretty pedigrees like them could never take on the angry, savage Alley cats. Not unless Bull was around.

After a moment, Fidel ordered Bait and his pack to rearrange his precious pillows back into a high mountain. Bait got off to a good start, but viciously began attacking a long string attached to one of the more scraggly ones. Seeing this battle, Cheeseburger seized the opportunity for some fun and lunged forward, landing on Bait. He emerged victoriously, the string now happily woven between his two front teeth.

"Cut it out, you imbeciles!" Fidel shouted loud enough to rattle Mr. Shadow's box.

Bait and Cheeseburger returned to the task at hand. The other Alleys went back to their original posts. Max continued to fill Fidel in on everything that happened while he was at the bar.

"They ran in here all of a sudden from all different doors and windows, almost like dey knew the joint," Max began.

"Interesting, interesting. Go on," Fidel said rubbing his chin.

"Well, they started barkin' and all, only it was pretty wimpy if you ask me," he snickered. "We all was hissin' and runnin' around, too. Dat's when Bait went crazy and stormed outta here looking for you. Anyways, a few dogs tried jumpin' on us and stuff, but Cheeseburger went into attack mode, and the dogs got real scared. They hid under the pillows. It was pretty funny stuff."

Fidel walked in a circle looking quite deep in thought. Rubbing his eyes, he sat down on the unstuffed couch.

"What is it, boss?" Max asked. "What are you thinkin' so hard about?"

Fidel spoke slowly and clearly. "I wonder why they attacked. What could five pampered pooches have wanted? They had to know they would never get rid of us."

But before Max could respond, Bait called from across the room. "Fidel? Fidel? You better come over here and get a look at dis."

With a large huff, Fidel met Bait. "What is it?" he snapped.

"See for yourself, boss."

Fidel looked down. There on the floor was a sixth dog, dead. A little Basset Hound, it looked as though its chest was crushed during the attack. His eyes were wide open, and his white and brown fur matted in a bloody mess.

"Drag him outta here before he wakes up," Fink suggested.

Slapping him across the head for the idiot he was, Fidel said, "He won't wake up, you moron! He's a dog! They don't have nine lives like us! They don't even have two lives!" Deciding it wasn't safe having a dead dog laying around, Fidel ordered its immediate disposal. Aside from the obvious reasons, the smell of the rotting carcass would soon become unbearable. "Throw him out back," he instructed his silent gang from the shadows. "Some stupid garbage man will have a nice surprise in the morning." As they were told, the five Alleys removed the dead Bassett and disposed of him in the trash.

"I can't believe I was taken away from my date for this! A bunch of wimpy, no-good, sissy dogs!" Fidel roared in Bait's direction. "You couldn't handle this one on your own? Huh? What am I training you guys for anyway?"

One by one, each Alley shamefully dropped its head. Pleasing Fidel was a task nobody would ever master.

Suddenly, Fidel caught Honey's female eye and realized Candle had still not returned. Always angry at losing an Alley, no matter how insignificant to his cause, he began to boil. "Where's Candle? She still not back?"

"Uh, sorry..boss. Nobody's seen her," Bait meekly said. "Maybe she went out for a walk or somethin' like..."

"Do you think I'm dumb?" Fidel howled. "She doesn't go for walks. She doesn't do anything! If she's not back tomorrow, there's going to be trouble!"

Nervously, everyone moved to the farthest corners of the room. Above them, Mr. Shadow cowered in his box.

In the library, Snickers, Uncle Fred, Mr. Sox, and the other hostage Sticks waited for a miracle.

Chapter Ten

That very night Romeo watched television nuzzled in Dennis's arms. They cozily sat on the couch trying to stay warm. Though the windows were closed, the cold outside air somehow seemed warmer than the apartment itself. Due to circumstances and the high price of oil, Mr. Crumb had been unable to pay the heating bill. Mrs. Crumb was already sneezing.

Although Dennis was thrilled to have Romeo home, he was terribly worried about his health. He carefully examined his badly beaten and swollen body. His breathing seemed wheezy and choppy. Judging by the severity of his wounds, Dennis thought perhaps he had been in a dogfight. Feeling incredibly guilty for Romeo's latest string of bad luck, Dennis vowed to keep him inside for a few days, or at least until he got better. Unaware of any of this, Romeo relaxed for the evening holding to the assumption he'd be back in Vent City tomorrow to meet his father, regardless of his body aches. He'd be up all night dreaming of the wondrous times they'd have together once Fidel was out of the picture. At noon, he and Fluffy would meet on the corner and begin the journey to Vent City again. For now, Romeo savored all the attention he could get from Dennis, hoping to soon see Pierre arrive home with some good news about the Factory. Maybe, just maybe, everything would be fine in the morning.

Late into the night, Dennis and Romeo were still sitting in front of the TV. Instead of doing his homework, Dennis laughed at the same old reruns when a news flash suddenly interrupted.

"This just in...," Bob, the nightly reporter, began, "The catnapper has been caught. I repeat, the catnapper has been caught. Sources tell me that earlier this evening, around eight o'clock, Buggles Flannigan was apprehended at his apartment by Sergeants Onion and Talbert. Apparently, the apartment was a small, garbage-infested pit that smelled really bad. Mr. Flannigan was brought directly to the station for questioning. Found in his dwelling was Calvin, the young kitten, tired and hungry but thankfully unharmed. Sources say Buggles Flannigan was to meet Lloyd, the pet's owner, tomorrow to collect his ransom totaling three thousand dollars. The call was traced after a late night phone call Lloyd received from the criminal himself. Officers moved in immediately. Buggles is being connected to last year's three bank robberies in which three city banks were held up at gunpoint. Buggles and his incarcerated partner, George MacNabber, got away with over ten thousand dollars cash. Mr. Flannigan is now being held on fifty thousand dollars bail and is expected to make his first court appearance on both catnapping and robbery charges later next week. As for Calvin the cat, he has safely returned home to his owner. Tune in tomorrow for our exclusive interview with Lloyd and his now famous cat..."

Dennis threw a cookie at the set, smashing it to pieces, as Romeo sat completely dumbfounded. Calvin, who only days earlier on the island truly believed he was a swarm of killer bees and a mad gorilla thanks to a hallucinatory plant, was now being hailed as famous! Just as Romeo was feeling the relief of Calvin's safe return, Dennis suddenly dropped a colossal bomb. "I think I'll take you to the Vet tomorrow, Romeo," Dennis whispered into the remote. "You look just awful, and I want to be one hundred percent sure you're going to be alright."

"Meow," Romeo pleaded. He couldn't go. He had a date with destiny. Sure he felt lousy, but the Vet? Never.

"I know you hate the Vet, Romeo, but it will

only take a few minutes. And I promise it won't hurt a bit," Dennis said, almost as if he understood Romeo's thoughts. "In fact, I went to the doctor last week. I only had one shot and it really didn't hurt at all. Honest," he added, fingers crossed behind his back. "Besides, I got a lollipop. Grape. It was the best thing I ate all week." Standing up, he stretched his boyish body to the ceiling, yawning wide. "Yep, it's settled. Tomorrow we go to the Vet."

Romeo watched Dennis walk down the hall and turn into his room. Going to the Vet was certainly something Romeo neither had the time nor the desire to do. Sure, he was messed up, but he'd be fine. It would just take time. That night, Romeo slept on the couch hoping to catch Pierre as he crawled through the window. Pierre liked using the window near the couch.

Despite all he had to think about, Romeo quickly drifted off to sleep. The apartment was cold, quite cold. Nuzzled in Grandma Crumb's wonderfully crocheted blanket, he started to snore, his little nostrils flaring. His mind, already plagued with enough stress and worry to fill the city, wasted no time sending him on a turbulent roller coaster ride. His nightmare first sent him spinning back to the island, devilishly reliving those few horrendous days, haunted by the image of Twitch's floating dead body. Next the dream took him to the Factory where Fidel made everyone dress up in clown suits and jump from a high wire onto the hard, wooden floor below. Suddenly Romeo's nightmare partnered him with Calvin and the bank robber as they staged a dangerous heist at the city's most prominent bank. There he was, gun in hand, bandana tied across his face. Grabbing bushels of money, Buggles the bank robber suddenly riddled Romeo and Calvin full of bullets, their blood splattering everywhere. The Pound carried them away, finally dumping their bodies into a large vent. They plummeted down a long tunnel and landed in a boiling pool of toxic waste. Romeo scrambled and struggled, as Calvin slowly slipped into the waste, his eyes going under last. Romeo's dream somehow found him at the Vet. There he lay in a completely white room, needles and sharp knives all around him. Five large, masked, mumbling men entered. Behind those masks were the most grisly, horrifying faces he'd ever seen, almost like something out of Vent City's elite. One ghastly face started to talk as he tightly held a large, pointy pair of scissors. "Romeo? Romeo? I've got to tell you something, Romeo!" it said. Suddenly, he felt a tug at his ear and instantly snapped out of his slumber, landing face to face with Pierre. "I've got to tell you something, Romeo," Pierre muttered again.

"Wha..? Wha..? What's happening? Don't hurt me!" Romeo spouted, still half asleep, covering his eyes with his paws.

Pierre looked at him as though he was

completely nuts. "*Mon Dieu,* you cats get weirder everyday. I swear."

"Pierre! Are the Alleys gone? Did you get Fidel out?" Romeo asked quickly, jolting out of his nightmare.

"Listen, Romeo," Pierre hesitantly continued, "we tried. We really did. But zose Alleys are just too mean, even for *moi*."

"What? What? Are you telling me you didn't get rid of them?" Romeo blurted. "They're still at the Factory?"

"Get rid of them? We *barely* came out alive! Zose cats are animals! Animals, I tell you! In fact, one of my pals is missing. Look Romeo, we went in like we practiced, *oui*? But zey cornered us right away! Zey even laughed at us! It was awful! Awful!" Pierre cried in his excited French accent.

"You've got to go back, Pierre! You've got to find a way! Cats are afraid of dogs!" Romeo reminded him.

"Forget it, Romeo!" Pierre shouted. "I'm never going back there again! *Jamais*! Zis was a stupid plan, a dangerous plan, and I don't really like you anyways. I think you set me up to get rid of me. *Oui,* that's it! You're in on za whole Alley thing, aren't you?"

"What? You can't be serious!" Romeo blundered.

"Of course, I see it now," Pierre went on

passionately. "You're a dog killer! Get away from me! Get away! *Alley*!" Pierre dashed down the hall, quickly running to the comfort he found under Dennis's bed.

Feeling awfully confused, Romeo slid beneath his orange crocheted blanket. He drifted back to sleep out of sheer exhaustion.

Wednesday morning began with the familiar ding of a thousand toasters and the howling whistle of boiling teakettles. Scores of city people hustled off to work, praying not to be greeted by a pink slip and a sweaty "good luck" handshake. A new mayor would be installed, one not favored by most. While Crowman, before his death, didn't accomplish much to improve society and better the system, he at least kept people working. Rumor had it Mr. Hashback wouldn't. Mr. Hashback, the new appointee, entered City Hall with a dark cloud over his head since he was a suspect in the Crowman murder case.

In the Crumb household Romeo awoke to the sizzling sound of three day old bacon, not to mention the worry and hope of what this new day would bring. He sat on the couch debating whether or not to escape before Dennis finished his morning bath. Although Romeo was heavily under-the-weather, his raging fever deluded him into thinking Dennis had forgotten the whole, crazy Vet idea. It was already nine, and school had begun. But unable to even lift his heavy head, Romeo lay in front of his food bowl growing more and more queasy at the sight of his dried tuna nuggets. His entire body ached much more than yesterday and he shivered all over.

Pierre had not emerged from Dennis's room, not even for the tin of crispy bacon fat awaiting him in the kitchen. In fact, it would be some time before he could face Romeo again. His irrational fear that Romeo was out to get him left him believing the worst-case scenario imaginable. Impressive how traumatizing the Alleys could be.

Staggering back to the couch, Romeo heard Dennis and his mother from the other room. "As soon as you're back from the Vet," Mrs. Crumb explained as she flattened her son's messy hair, "you run right off to school. I don't want you missing too much, you understand?"

"Yes, but what about Romeo? He's really sick!" Dennis warned. "I should stay home with him."

Mrs. Crumb paused, checking her aging reflection in Dennis's window. "I'll be here if he needs looking after. Besides, I'm sure he's fine. He's a tough one, remember? After all, this is Romeo you're talking about."

Dennis smiled at her words of confidence.

"Now, you run ahead. I've already called the

school. They're going to tell your teacher you'll be late. Don't forget to have the Vet send the bill to me, and don't buy any medicines until I speak to your father about it. Now, run along. I'll be expecting you back soon."

Dennis left his bedroom dressed and ready, math homework ripped in half and stuffed between his two front pockets. In his right hand was his yellow rain hat and in his left was the cat carrier. Used only in extreme emergencies or Vet visits, its blue plastic walls surrounded the cramped, lonely space Romeo would soon become so intimate with. At the front of the box, a door of stainless steel prison bars allowed in only small glimpses of the outside world. Romeo dove behind a pillow, burying himself into the tight corner where the back of the sofa met the cushions.

"Come here, Romeo," Dennis said persuasively. "Come on! Good boy! Here's your box!"

"Hissss," Romeo growled in his most ferocious voice.

"Now, now, Romeo, be brave!"

Brave. Brave. That was something Romeo always dreamed he'd be. Brave. So to be truly brave, he allowed Dennis to grab him from between the cushions without much of a struggle. Dennis lifted him high into the air, his paws dangling effortlessly through the bacon scented air. To confirm his previous observations, Dennis inspected Romeo one last time to make sure he was actually sick. Satisfied with his diagnosis, Romeo was lowered into the box as it sat propped up on its side. Once in, Dennis quickly locked the door.

"You're brave, Romeo," Dennis said proudly. "Very brave."

Romeo squashed himself into the cold, confining corners of the box.

Meanwhile at the Factory, Fidel awoke to a concerto of snores. Every Alley around him lay slumped on the floor, noses running and sawing wood like crazy. The sound of all those plugged up nasal cavities sliced through his brain like nails to a chalkboard. He waited for a moment, allowing his crew their needed sleep. After all, energy was the key to their success, and sleep was the key to energy. But after covering his ears with two pillows and still writhing from the annoying wheezes, he had finally enough. "Wake up! Wake up, Alleys!" he exploded. "Wake up!"

Deep in his recurring dream involving a pool sized bowl of tuna, Bait catapulted at the crack of Fidel's voice, bumping his head hard on the underside of a wooden chair. "Ouch!" he wailed, still paddling through the imagined tuna.

"Hey, what's the big idea?" Max shouted. "Why's you wakin' us up so early, boss?"

Fidel looked around the room, happy to see his faithful silent five ready for action at the base of his cotton stuffed castle. "I said wake up you miserable bunch!" he hollered to the lazy ones still asleep.

A low grumble hovered over the room.

"It's going to be a busy day," Fidel announced, not wasting a second. "Max, you're to lead the search for Candle. Clank and Mustard, let me know how the hostages are doing upstairs. See to it that they're *miserable,*" he added, devilishly rubbing his smelly paws together. "Make sure Steak is keeping an eye on them! Don't screw up! Do I make myself clear?"

"Ay-ay, captain," Clink and Mustard saluted, dashing up to the library.

Bait approached Fidel, still savoring the fleeting scent of tuna in his head. "Hey, Fidel, I thought I was lookin' for Candle."

Fidel looked up and snapped, "Look at you, Bait! You're pathetic! Max is taking over. Besides, I got another job for you."

"Fidel, I really got stuff to do at the Glitterbox," Max huffed. "Maybe Bait could find..."

"Later, Max. You can do that later," Fidel interrupted. "We'll go there together. I have to find Raven anyway. For now, you'll find Candle. That's an order!"

"Then what'll I do?" Bait asked, nuzzling up to a fluffy pillow.

"Look for Romeo!" Fidel reminded, knocking him awake. "As for the rest of you, enjoy your new home!" he surprisingly announced.

Chapter Nine

"Yeah!" the Alleys cheered, the silent five nodding their heads coolly. Bait, on the other hand, sat up, disgruntled and bitter.

"Why can't I relax and enjoy?" he asked himself. "This blows."

In need of some laughs, Bait decided to cheer himself up with a poke or two at Mr. Shadow. Seeing Shadow shiver was always good fun. Stalking across a high rafter, Bait slithered to Mr. Shadow's box. He slowly stretched his left paw over the edge and rattled the cage. No scream. Nothing. Leaning over the beam, Bait looked in. The box was empty! "Fidel! Fidel! Come quick!" he shouted, tipping the box on its side.

"Oh, what is it now, Bait?" Fidel growled. "Cheeseburger and I are having an important meeting!"

"He's gone! Shadow is gone!" Bait wailed. "Disappeared! Vanished!"

"What do you mean, he's gone?" Fidel hollered.

"He's just gone! That's all there is to it!"

"This is an outrage! How could this have happened?" Fidel cried in a foaming mess. "Find him, Bait! Everybody, get up! Search! We must find Shadow now, or else!"

"Oh, just let him go, Fidel," Max shouted, grabbing Fidel by the shoulders. "He's worthless anyway. We got enough to do around here without lookin' for that cripple."

"Are you crazy? Let him go?" Fidel cracked. "I'm not letting *anybody* go! Find him I say! Find all of them! Do it or get out!" With that, he got right in Max's face. "And don't forget who's boss, *Max*! What I say goes, got it? Or do you need to be taught a lesson?"

"Okay, sorry. We're on it, boss." Max prepared himself for yet another hopeless search, forever longing to return to his thriving club. Above his head, the vacant box swung by its ropes. Unbeknownst to anyone, Jailbird lay fast asleep under a pillow, strangely exhausted and out of commission.

Chapter Eleven

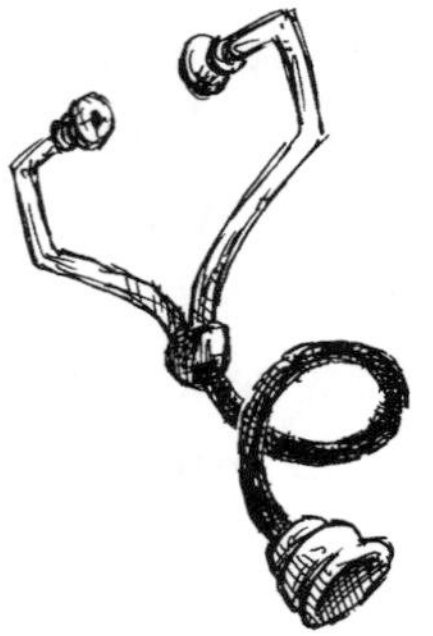

It took twenty minutes for Dennis to walk to the Vet. Twenty long minutes. With every jiggly step, Romeo bounced and rolled in his tiny box. In no time, it had begun to rain. At least Romeo managed to remain fairly dry.

Romeo shut his eyes as Dennis splashed through the puddles. Unlike most people, Dennis enjoyed the rain, not only for its effect on his dreaded little league games, but for the simplicity of it. He loved feeling it drip down his face as he looked up at the clouds, drops falling in his mouth and hiding under his coat. The rain's smell awoke in him the little boy who still loved playing in the mud and dancing in the deep, deep puddles. If he could live out his boyish fantasy, he'd dive in and swim around town like a fish.

Looking out between the little jail bars, Romeo

saw the large, familiar building before him. He recognized the jagged, arrow-shaped crack in the big glass doors. Up on the third floor was the Vet's clinic, along with the sinking feeling of panic.

Dennis left Romeo alone on an orange plastic chair as he checked in with the receptionist. "Romeo Crumb for Dr. Stein," Dennis said politely. "We have an appointment."

"The doctor will be with you shortly," she said with as much enthusiasm as the orange chair.

Huddled in the far corner of his box, Romeo could hear the pathetic wails and cries of the other sad patients in the waiting room. Each sounded more pitiful and wretched than the next. Some dogs, some cats, a bird, even a tarantula. Regardless of the fact they were practically all enemies, when in this place they shared a common bond, a knowing fear that comes with being a pet. All around him Romeo smelled the antiseptic sting that lingered in every doctor's office. It made him all the more tense and nervous and in constant wonderment of what probing and prodding examination he would have to endure. Despite his anxiety, he nearly fell asleep for he was growing weaker and more tired from his sickly state. In fact, by the time the nurse called his name, he could barely open his eyes.

"Right this way," she droned, leading Dennis through the white but fingerprinted swinging doors. "Room six."

Chapter Eleven

Like a good cat, Romeo prayed that Bubastis would be with him in this desperate time of need, there to protect him from the unspeakable dangers haunting the everlasting hallways leading to the Vet.

"What a cutie pie!" shrieked a woman's voice. "Goo-goo-goo-goo!" she teased, shoving her fingers through the metal bars of Romeo's cage.

"His name's Romeo," Dennis proudly said as he entered the examination room.

"Well, isn't he just the sweetest little-bitty thing I've ever seen?" the woman continued in an annoying baby voice.

Swatting the long, red nails out of his way, Romeo glared between the bars and found the round, chubby face of one of the nurses. "Hello in there, little guy!" she smiled, giving off the enticing scent of huevos rancheros. "Did you try to bite my finger, you little sly one?" She looked him over one last time. "You've got a special guy here, Dennis."

Dennis put the cage on the examining table. Romeo swore he could feel the cold of the metal table seeping through the box and into his bones. He shivered and shook some fur right off his body. When the door suddenly unlocked, Romeo glued himself to the far end of the cage, clutching desperately to the walls. Like an evil demon, Dennis tipped the cage over, forcing Romeo onto the aluminum silver tabletop. Below him, his distorted reflection stared back at him in a blurred, nightmarish blob.

"Now Romeo, why are you so scared? Dr. Stein's not going to hurt you," Dennis assured lovingly, holding Romeo's shaking body close and petting his head.

"Meoooow," Romeo purred sadly.

After what seemed like hours of staring at the cat posters, sterile instruments, and medicine bottles, the doorknob turned. In walked Dr. Stein. He still sported the same stupid, little beard and one gold hoop earring. Romeo could almost feel his cold hands reaching around his belly, doing things he'd rather not remember, even before he touched him.

"Good morning, Dennis," Dr. Stein greeted, shaking Dennis's hand. "How's our little fella doing?"

"Not so good, Dr. Stein," Dennis said. "He's sick or something."

"Well, let's just take a look, shall we?"

Stethoscope dangling in front of him, Romeo suddenly felt those same cold hands reaching around his bruised body. He lunged for Dennis's raincoat but was immediately flipped on his back, tickled and inspected, the bright light above shinning in his little eyes. Back on his belly, Dr. Stein quickly shoved something in his right ear, then his left! Then he did the same to his eyes! What was he looking for? Romeo scrambled around on the table, his fur clinging to the sweat forming on the metal. He knew Dennis and the doctor were talking, though he couldn't hear anything above the hum in his head. Then it happened. He felt a chilling, object slip in his bottom. *It's all over now,* Romeo thought. *This is the end.* But before he knew it, the object was soon gone. With Dennis's help, Romeo was held down so he couldn't move. He saw a long, sharp needle heading for his backside. It was probably for some horrible medical experiment! *This must have been how it was for Twitch,* Romeo thought. *Disastrous. How could Dennis do this to me?* Romeo howled at the top of his lungs as the sharp needle pierced his flesh.

After all the scary procedures, Romeo heard the doctor finally say, "Very good, Romeo. It's all over."

Romeo opened his eyes to see Dennis and the doctor smiling as they each stroked his sweaty back. The sight of all those gruesome tools on the table sent Romeo flying back into the safe corner of his cage, which he now loved more than anything.

"Well, doc, is that it?" Dennis asked with concern.

"Dennis, he has a slight fever," Dr. Stein began, "but his ears are clear and his vision is fine. The bumps you see are probably from a catfight. A pretty bad one at that. The antibiotic shot I gave him will help heal up the scratches, but he'll need to take two pills every four hours for the next week or his fever will rise, which could get dangerous. *Very* dangerous," he warned with one raised eyebrow. "We don't want his lungs filling up. If he gets pneumonia, he may not make it."

Dennis remembered what his mother said about buying medicines. "How much will the pills cost?"

"About eighty-five dollars. Expensive, but very necessary. Have your father call me from work and we'll see what we can work out."

"Oh, Lord," Dennis whispered. "Eighty-five dollars?"

Once home, Romeo was put on the couch as Dennis explained the dire situation to his mother. "Please, mom," he cried, "Dr. Stein said Romeo might die without it! We have to get that medicine!"

Mrs. Crumb looked up from her needlepoint. "I don't know, Dennis, eighty-five dollars is an awful lot of money to spend on a cat. We need that money for ourselves. We'll just have to wait for your father to come home."

"But that could be too late! The vet will be closed, and he needs those pills today! By tomorrow he could be sicker!" Dennis urged desperately.

"I'm sorry, Dennis, there's nothing else I can do. Now, run along to school. Don't worry, I'll watch the cat."

The cat. The cat. Those words rang in Romeo's head. He was more than just *the cat*. Dennis knew that. Anyone who used words like *the cat* wasn't about to spend eighty-five dollars on some lousy pills. Romeo knew he was in trouble, big trouble. Losing a life like this would be too painful for everyone. If Dennis saw him die, how could he go on living with him? Dennis didn't know about the nine lives. To all humans, that concept was only a myth. Romeo had to do something. He couldn't die in front of Dennis. *I know, I'll get out of here. If I don't get better, I'll die outside somewhere. Then I'll wake up and Dennis will think I just got healthy again. But wait! I don't want to die! I simply can't! What if an Alley finds me when I'm dead? Oh, I'm thinking crazy. This is never going to work. What will I do?* The words spun in Romeo's head like a whirlpool.

"Don't worry, Romeo," Dennis whispered almost as if he could hear Romeo's thoughts. "Dad will buy you those pills. He has to. You just rest until he gets home." In a flash Dennis hurried out the door and off to school.

With a sigh of relief, Romeo rested on the couch believing Dennis's words. Of course they'd buy him the pills. The Crumbs liked keeping their son happy. That's why they bought Romeo and Pierre in the first place. The last thing they'd do is let his kitty die. Romeo didn't need to worry about it at all. Still, he was feeling worse by the moment. The shot the doctor gave him was wearing off and he could feel the pounding in his body return. Almost like a real nip addict, he longed for those pills. Mrs. Crumb gently petted him on the back as he slowly drifted off to sleep.

As noon approached, Fluffy, unaware of Romeo's doctor visit, met up with Darla and headed for the corner to meet Romeo as planned. Luckily, Fluffy hadn't gotten quite as sick as Romeo.

"I can't believe that whole story," Darla went on. "The toxic waste, poor Mr. Gamble, and all those creepy animals! I'm sorry I split when I did."

Darla explained that as the fight with the rats erupted, she saw her chance for escape and took it assuming Romeo and Fluffy would follow close behind. After waiting two whole hours at the vent, she imagined the worst and ran home all alone.

As they waited for Romeo, they reminisced about their Stick friends and wondered how they were. "I'd really like to see Snickers and Uncle Fred," Fluffy said with a sigh. "You know, as quirky as they are, I really do miss them."

"Yeah, they're good guys," Darla agreed.

"And poor Mr. Sox. What I wouldn't give to talk to him right now," Fluffy added.

Darla blinked her eyes and sat down. "I miss Tabitha the most. Since you guys got back from the island, she hasn't even left her room. I've tried, but I can't get her to come out."

"What about Soot, Ms. Purrpurr, Waffles and Vittles, Roy and Yellowtail, MayBelle, and now Mr. Shadow?" Fluffy whimpered. "It just makes me so sad."

Patting Fluffy on the back, Darla looked sadly into his eyes. "They're alright, Fluffy. True, they're captives, but hopefully they're healthy and on their way to going home. I bet they miss you too, and I know they'd be really proud of you and Romeo."

"Thanks, Darla," Fluffy said with a little grin.

When the clock on a nearby deli wall said twelve-thirty, Fluffy and Darla began to get worried. It wasn't like Romeo to be late, especially when it was something as important as seeing his father again. Anxious and eager, Fluffy decided to climb up to Romeo's window while Darla continued to wait outside. Though pretty banged up himself, he could still make it the five stories.

"If you see anyone suspicious, just run home," Fluffy warned. "Don't worry about me, just get yourself to safety. Got it?"

"Yes, Fluffy," she agreed. "But I'm sure I'll be fine. There are a lot of people out today, and I'm positive I'll be here when you get back. If you don't see me, it's just because I had to pee or something."

"Okay," Fluffy responded.

While Darla stood in the rain, Fluffy pounded up Romeo's building with purpose. Knowing exactly where to go, he immediately found Dennis's window and peeked inside. Gluing himself to the glass, he saw Pierre oddly parading around on the sock splattered floor. He had on a tiny cowboy hat and a pair of Dennis's white underwear, his tail sticking out one of the legs. Around his neck was a big, green ribbon from Mrs. Crumbs' sewing basket, and on his paws he had shoes molded of tinfoil. He was dancing to some old tune in front of the mirror when Fluffy knocked on the glass.

"Hey, Frenchie, what the heck's going on in there?" Fluffy yelled.

"*Zute*!" Pierre shouted, flinging his costume around the room. "Uh...uh, Dennis makes me do this. He hopes that one day I'll...hey, wait a minute. Who are you anyway?"

"I'm Romeo's friend. Where is he?" Fluffy slowly mouthed, swatting his ribbons out of the way. "He was supposed to meet us."

Pierre hopped up to the window, quickly shoving his cowboy hat under the desk. "He can't meet you. He just came back from the Vet with Dennis, *oui*? Now he's knocked out on the couch. Can't go in there. The mama's with him."

"The Vet? The Vet? You're kidding! He must really be sick," Fluffy said with concern.

Pierre opened the window so he didn't have to shout, although he did love yelling at cats. "That's what I said. Look, I have *beaucoup* stuff to do. So, why don't you scram!" Slamming the window shut, he leapt off the desk and gathered his tinfoil shoes together where Fluffy couldn't see.

Back at the street corner, Fluffy explained everything to Darla. "We'll just have to go it alone," he told her.

"Without Romeo?" she asked. "That wouldn't be right!"

Chapter Eleven

"What choice have we got? It's go alone or risk wasting more precious time. Let's do it for Romeo."

Fluffy and Darla forged ahead, finding their way back to Vent City, keeping Romeo in their thoughts. On their arrival, they narrowly missed the rats by hiding behind a large, wooden block. To their delight, they quickly found Mr. Gamble and immediately told him of Romeo's illness.

"My heavens, is he going to be alright?" Mr. Gamble questioned immediately.

"I'm sure there's nothing to worry about," Fluffy explained. "You saw him yesterday and he looked no worse off than me. And he's been to the Vet! But Mr. Gamble, I know Romeo wanted to tell you his idea about Fidel. I really would like to..."

"Of course, Fluffy, of course. I'm sure it's a wonderful idea, but we've got a lot of work to do."

"But, Mr. Gamble..."

"There'll be time later to tell me about his little plan. I won't forget." Mr. Gamble led Fluffy and Darla down the long, damp hallway. As they walked Darla turned her head to see the large boulder that kept Candle locked away from the rest of the world. She was still in there, alone. *She's an Alley,* Darla said to calm herself. *She doesn't matter.*

Eventually Mr. Gamble took them to the meeting room where Fluffy and Romeo had been the day before. The usuals were there, Chester, the morbidly, boneless dog, Hayward and his nauseating eyes, Bradley, George, Wanda, the mutated cat/roach, just to name a few. As Darla looked at them for the very first time, her stomach flew out of her body and she felt herself racing toward the exit. "Get me outta here!" she wailed. "These things are worse than I thought! Help!"

"Darla, wait! Come back! Come back!" On his sore legs, Fluffy dashed after her, finally tackling her to the ground. She struggled to break free. "Look Darla, I'm scared of these guys, too, but, they didn't hurt any of us yesterday, not after they knew who we were. They're okay."

"I can't! I can't!" she cried, scrambling to her feet. "Look at them!"

"You've got to! We've come this far!" Fluffy yelled, shaking her hand.

Suddenly Myrna came hobbling up. "Don't worry about us, honey. You can stay." Her grotesque features glistened under the hazy light, little bits of goop dripping from her flesh onto the ground.

"What was that? It's...it's an alien!" Darla screamed nervously.

"These two are wasting our time, Mr. G," George whined, spitting his smelly breath in everyone's face. "Do they have to be here? We've got important work to do!"

"They're not going to bother you. They'll be quiet. I promise," Mr. Gamble assured. "Now Darla, please come inside. You can meet everybody, and you'll see, things are going to be just fine. They just take some getting used to. Soon their good kind souls will make you forget their unfortunate exteriors."

Helping Darla into the meeting room, Fluffy fanned her sweaty brow and held her trembling paw. Like Romeo and Fluffy, she too was formally introduced to everyone, though it did little to ease her nerves. Even Fluffy was getting creeped out again. Things were definitely not the same without Romeo there.

Soon the meeting resumed. It was a very crucial and busy time for the Vent City animals, hardly time for making new friendships. Only a few days away from the most awaited moment of their lives, everyone bonded together. Though tense and nervous, they held pep-rallies, studied and restudied maps and strategies of the city. Mr. Gamble hardly had a moment to visit with Fluffy and Darla. Everyone needed his last minute approval on this decision or that one. Not only were the main team members involved, but soon other strange creatures crawled out of their caves and boxes and joined in the action. After sitting and watching for a while in the corner, Fluffy asked a question.

"Mr. Gamble, can we help?" he said still adorned in his frayed little bows. "I mean, are you really going to get the Alleys out of the Factory? Will our Stick friends really be alright?"

"Factory? Factory? What are you talking

about?" Mr. Gamble questioned.

Fluffy looked straight at Darla. "Well, *surely* you know about Fidel taking over the Factory with all our friends as his captives. You must know. Don't you? I mean, that's why we're here, right?"

"No!" Mr. Gamble began to pace about the room. "Why didn't you tell me this before?"

"I tried to tell you. So did Romeo. Remember his idea about Fidel?" Fluffy whined. "We thought you knew. How could you know about the island and not about Fidel and the Factory?"

Mr. Gamble froze deep in thought. "Romeo and I only talked about me and the toxic waste tragedy. Besides, I haven't been out in the city at all lately. It's been too dangerous. I sent a spy to wait for you by the dock. He told me you'd arrived safely but mentioned nothing about this Fidel-Factory situation."

"Well, Mr. Gamble, what are you going to do now?" Darla asked, still studying the monsters around her.

"It all makes sense now. Fluffy, Darla, this news changes everything," Mr. Gamble went on. "I've got to see Romeo. It's time to get you guys involved."

Later that day under a blanket of used tissues, Romeo stirred. Feverish, he had been passed out on the couch for hours. At school Dennis sat all day at his desk helpless with thoughts of Romeo and his needed medicine. Mr. Crumb, spending another exhausting day on the job, took the long walk home again. Mrs. Crumb watched a marathon of soap operas, wondering why her life never became as glamorous as the characters on the screen. She used a whole box of tissue sneezing away her cold symptoms and tragic storylines. Pierre, perhaps the only one having a good day, went on practicing his routines dressed in Dennis's things.

By the time Dennis finally arrived home, Romeo was awake but hardly looking any better. In fact, he looked worse.

"Your father should be home soon," Mrs. Crumb said, gathering her tissues off the ground. "He stopped at the bar for a drink after work, I'm sure of it."

"Did he get Romeo's pills?" Dennis asked nervously.

"I don't know. I'm sure everything will be fine, though," she reassured him.

Dennis reached over to pat Romeo's little head. It was bumpy and sweaty, his eyes red and tired. Obviously, he wasn't getting any better. Dr. Stein's words haunted Dennis, "...it could get very dangerous. He needs that medicine..." Waiting nervously on the couch for his father's return, Dennis cradled Romeo in his arms as his mother opened a new box of tissue.

Chapter Eleven

After a string of bad sitcoms, the evening news broke in with an exciting update on their top story.

"Here we are at Lloyd's apartment where we left you yesterday with this riveting saga," Bob, the reporter, began. "Today, not only are cat and owner happy and resettled together, but we have just learned that Calvin, Lloyd's brave feline companion, is actually an actor himself! In fact, he was the inspiring cat of the Gritty Kitty Pee Removal Kit's last campaign before the company went under from the Crowman Day Parade balloon fiasco."

From the warmth of Dennis's arm, Romeo sat up straight and tall, his ears all a twitter.

"...Join us now as Lloyd and Calvin perform a scene from the runaway smash hit, 'My Darling Maudie'," Reporter Bob delighted.

With good intentions, Lloyd and Calvin attempted to reproduce this famous musical right there on the news, but lacked the obvious talent to do so. Pathetically parading around the drabby apartment in front of the cameras and the world, Calvin and Lloyd fully embarrassed not only themselves, but all out of work actors alike, human and animal. "Are they all that bad?" thought the rest of the thinking world. "Or just the ones with cats?" While Calvin performed for stale kitty treats, the news crew gawked and snickered behind their backs. As always, Lloyd hoped his star cat would gain him some notoriety and a spec of the limelight, especially since the unfortunate catnapping. If this didn't do it, nothing would.

I can't believe this, Romeo said to himself. *As lousy as he is, Calvin's famous! He really did it! I bet the whole kidnapping thing was a hoax just to get on TV!*

Romeo listened as Bob retook the mike. "Join us for our on-going coverage as we reveal the secrets behind this 'talented' duo and talk openly with cat psychologist, Wayne Whittle. Also, we will continue to update you on Buggles, the infamous catnapper. Authorities are investigating his link to our citywide disappearing cat situation. Over twenty-five pet cats have been reported missing to date."

Just as Romeo was about to retake his warm spot on the couch, the front doorknob turned. When Mr. Crumb opened the door to come in, a cold draft whipped passed him, swirling around the room like an unwanted guest. For the first time ever, Dennis noticed his father stumbling like the homeless men who hung around the school yard at lunch. Mrs. Crumb recognized his smell, immediately shooting him a sure-fire sobering look. "You're drunk, aren't you?" she whispered, somehow believing Dennis didn't hear her. "How could you?"

Feeling uncomfortable, Dennis grabbed his backpack and began emptying his books onto the floor. Whichever fell out first would be the one he'd open. "Drat! Math," he said into the bag.

While Mr. and Mrs. Crumb went into the

kitchen to argue, Dennis began to feel more and more the way he did at Billy Radcliff's house. *Billy's* parents were always fighting, sometimes even hitting each other with magazines and stuff. That would never happen at Dennis's house. This he knew for sure. True, his parents were under a lot of financial stress lately, but they were good people. Despite his warm feelings toward them, he still hated to hear his parents argue, let alone see his father tipsy. It was something that never happened in his family, except when old Uncle Stewart, the garbage collector from Chinatown, came around. He drank a lot.

"What's happened to you?" Mrs. Crumb wailed from the other room. "I don't understand! You never used to drink."

"Yeah, well times have changed!" his father snapped back.

After some more garbled exchanges, Dennis quickly gathered his things together, picked up Romeo and ran into his room. At least there he was Dennis, just Dennis, not a kid with fighting parents. No matter what, he knew when they walked into his room they'd be the parents he'd always known and loved.

After a while, Dennis's mom and dad did come in, cheery as expected. This time Mr. Crumb reeked of strong coffee. Mrs. Crumb's eyes and nose were redder than they'd been from her long day of sneezing. "Listen, son," Mr. Crumb began with a hiccup, "I'm sorry you had to see that."

Dennis turned the page of his upside-down math book and bit his pencil hard.

"See, work's been tough lately, and well, you understand, don't you?" Mr. Crumb said kneeling down next to him.

"Sure, dad, I understand," Dennis reassured.

"It's just that I want to give you and your mother everything in the world and well, I can't seem to do that."

Dennis looked up from his homework, his face confused and sad. "I don't want everything, dad. I just want things to be normal."

"I do too," his dad added. "By the way, I didn't get a chance to call the Vet, but your mom tells me Romeo needs special medicine."

"Dad, Romeo's really sick. Dr. Stein said he could die without those pills. Can we get them tomorrow? I'll pick them up before school."

"Sure, son, but how much will they cost?" This was the question Dennis feared most. He gulped hard, almost hoping Romeo would start coughing or puking right in front of his dad for dramatic effect. "Eighty-five dollars," he said softly.

"Eighty-five dollars? Are you crazy?" his dad exploded. "You think I just have eighty-five dollars lying around? First you wanted reward money, now this? I'm sorry Dennis, but I can't do it! I know you love him, we all do, but I just don't have that kind of money!"

"But, dad, he'll get pneumonia and die!" Dennis pleaded. "What happened to giving me everything and all that junk?"

"We'll talk about this later," Mrs. Crumb said, implying when every drop of beer was out of her husband's system. "Romeo will be just fine tonight."

Mr. Crumb stumbled back to the kitchen for more coffee. Mrs. Crumb followed, leaving a trail of tissues behind her. Again they started to bicker, this time about money. It seemed nothing was going to get better for a long time.

Romeo stood framed in the doorway looking as if he was about to collapse.

Chapter Twelve

Back in Alley-ville, the search went on for Mr. Shadow and Candle. It wasn't going well, and no one but Steak still knew about Darla's daring escape. He was hoping to keep it that way.

Fidel stormed angrily up the back staircase to check on the Sticks in the library. He found them huddled together in one huge mass, scared and shaking pathetically.

"Shadow up here?" Fidel demanded, looking in Steak's direction as Steak darted frantically around the room for no apparent reason. "Steak! Get over here!"

"Yessir, Fidel."

"You're up here the most. Have you seen or heard *anything* about Shadow? Anything at all?" Fidel blustered.

Chapter Twelve

Shaking his head no while scratching his belly, Steak replied, "Nothin' unusual up here, boss."

"Well, someone must have helped him. Shadow couldn't walk outta here alone with those broken legs. When I find out who sprung him, I'll... I'll kill him!" Fidel thought out loud, twiddling his ID tags with his claw. Behind him, his silent five scoured the library looking for any possible clue to the Stick's mysterious disappearance.

"Mr. Shadow's free?" Uncle Fred roared triumphantly upon hearing the news. "You can't keep the rest of us here forever, Fidel!"

"Shush, Uncle Fred!" Mr. Sox jabbed in his direction. "Be quiet!"

"We're gonna get out and when we do, you'll be sorry!" Uncle Fred yelled maniacally, paying no attention to Mr. Sox.

"Shut up!" Mr. Sox demanded, this time pulling Fred by the tail.

Standing on all fours, Uncle Fred lifted his chin high and glared at Fidel in a state of mad delirium. "We're gonna get you, Fidel!"

"Stop it, Uncle Fred!" Waffles exploded. "You'll get us all in trouble!"

"Now that Darla *and* Mr. Shadow have escaped, it's just a matter of time for the rest of us! They're going to find Romeo and bust us outta here!" blared Uncle Fred as he dangled kicking and screaming from Waffle's angry grasp.

"Steak! Bait! What is he blabbing about?" Fidel thundered. "Another Stick escaped? And I was not informed?" In the corner Steak frantically scrambled for a hiding place, finally ducking under a shredded book jacket.

"I...I...didn't know, Fidel!" Bait groveled from the floor. "I swear! I swear!"

In a seething rage, Fidel ran up to Steak, ripped the book jacket off of his body and flung him up in the air. "Why did you not tell me about this? Answer me!"

"It's a funny thing, really," Steak cried nervously, sweat beads forming on his nose. "See, I was going to tell you, yeah, that's it, but I..."

"Look, Fidel," Mr. Sox interrupted bravely. "Why don't we discuss this like two civilized cats."

"You're no *cat*, Sox! You're just a Stick! And I hate Sticks!" Fidel scowled, cornering him against the wall. Mr. Sox stood silently with his nose to the ground. Despite the horror in the room, his elegance and dignity somehow remained perfectly in tact. He was the ultimate gentleman even in the face of grave danger.

"Mr. Sox, no!" cried Soot from the far corner of the room. "Leave him alone, Fidel!"

"I'll tell you what we're going to do," Fidel growled, still peering into Mr. Sox's troubled eyes. "Alleys, listen up! Every Stick here loses one life! Do it, Alleys! Now!"

Chapter Twelve

The Sticks flew into mass hysteria as the Alleys cheered and hollered. "You're da' best, Fidel!" Clink rallied on. "Three cheers for Fidel!"

"This is gonna be fun!" Mustard hollered, devilishly rubbing his paws together and seeking out his prey. "Hmm, where to begin."

"We've got to get out of here!" Soot cried under his breath. "We've got to find help!" The Sticks huddled closer together, bashing into each other.

"What about Mr. Sox? He's a niner! He can't die! He can't!" someone shouted from the back of the room.

"Too bad, Sticks! What I say goes!" Fidel shouted with a hiss. Not one Stick could have ever imagined such a vile, immoral defeat. In spite of their many downfalls, never had they been faced with such a monstrosity. "Have fun boys!" Fidel laughed as he headed for the door with his silent five close behind.

The Alleys marched forward like a brick wall of mean football players, drooling through their sharp teeth, their eyes swirling around in their sockets.

"Oh, the fe-lanity!" Snickers wailed from his belly, foam pouring from his mouth.

"Somebody help poor Mr. Sox!" MayBelle cried, tossing herself to the ground like a rabid dog. "He's a niner!"

By now the Alleys were enjoying the terror show play out on the ground as the Sticks became more and more frantic.

"Bait! You're coming with me!" Fidel motioned. He gave Snickers a last kick.

"What? Don't I get to have some fun too?" Bait whined.

"I said, you're coming with me! We've got work to do!"

Bait threw himself on his knees. "Awe, come on. Can I just get one of the little guys for fun? Can I, huh? Please?" he begged, showing off his rotting teeth.

"No!" screamed Fidel, savagely yanking Bait by the ear and throwing him out of the room. As Fidel shoved Bait down the stairs, he began to feel a rumble beneath his paws growing louder and louder, knocking Bait right off one of the steps.

"Wh..what's that?" Fidel asked, grabbing hold of the crackling banister. "No, it can't be..."

Suddenly, every last Stick exploded out of the library, pounding down the stairs and smashing right through the rec room door.

"Get them! Quick!" Fidel hollered from his flattened position on the steps.

But it was too late. Like a massive wind, the Sticks raced out of the Factory and into the streets without stopping for a breath. Running their separate ways, their whistles and howls echoed blocks away, filling the night air with their intoxicated energy. Nobody looked back.

"Damn them!" Fidel screamed. "Those Sticks

can't defy me! I'm the one in charge! Me!" Like a demon, he flew back up to the library to confront his inept soldiers.

Fidel exploded through the library door with a new felt fury that seeped through his pulsing veins burning a hole in his heart. Seething in rage, he stared at the wretched scene before him. At the center of the room was Max, the only Alley still standing. The rest of his sorry lot lay writhing and wiggling on the floor in unspeakable pain and torture. Covered in the noxious spray of mace, they clutched desperately to their burning eyes and bubbling skin. Their moans were unbearable. Paralyzed on the floor, they lay in a heaping pathetic mess. The Sticks had escaped.

"They didn't all get away," Max said, firmly holding Mr. Sox and Uncle Fred by their collars. "We's gots the slowest ones. Those other Sticks will be back for these guys. Especially the old one. You can be sure of it." Mr. Sox and Uncle Fred fought shamelessly in Max's clutches, longing to get out of there once and for all.

"Who did this?" Fidel thundered. "How did this happen?"

"It all happened so fast," Honey whimpered, frozen in the fetal position. "Nobody saw it coming."

"Let me at 'im! Let me at 'im!" another Alley howled from the back of the pile.

"It was the darndest thing, boss," Max said.

He was the only one not hit by the stinging mace.

"Max! Find out who did this and bring them to me! They couldn't have gone too far! Go!" Fidel hollered, biting at his claws in a rapid frenzy. "In the meantime, the rest of you losers get yourselves together and catch those blasted Sticks! Kill them dead if you have to! They can't escape me! And find Romeo! This is all his fault!"

Max threw Mr. Sox and Uncle Fred to the floor, immediately helping the Alleys back on their feet. Mr. Sox lay dizzy and bewildered on the cold ground until he caught a glimpse of two shiny objects off in the far, far corner of the library. He squinted tightly and found himself looking directly into Jailbird's eyes. Sitting alone and hidden in the shadowy darkness, he held a large metal can in his paws. Mr. Sox blinked, and he was gone.

Chapter Thirteeen

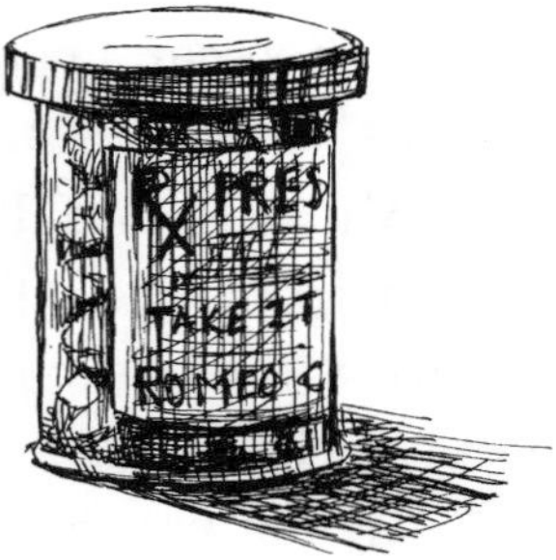

Romeo heard an unexpected knock on the window. Nuzzled under Dennis's legs and feeling worse by the hour, he repeatedly heard the loud banging on the frigid, frosty glass. Under the bed Pierre snored like an old man, one of his tin foil shoes pressed purposely against his mouth for some late night chewing. Afraid the Alleys had come back, Romeo decided to play it safe and head into another room. If the Alleys didn't see him with Dennis, they'd hopefully give up and leave.

Romeo carefully unstuck himself from between the back of Dennis's knees and the sheets. He peeked over the side of the bed. The window was closed but the curtains were opened just a sliver. Slinking in and out of the shadows on the floor, he headed for the living room and the bumpy couch where he had been all day. In the faint light of the doorway, Romeo could see scary silhouettes on the outside of the window as he marched down the long, dark hall. From under the bed Pierre's monotonous snoring followed him, even the irritating sound of his crackling tinfoil shoe.

Weak with fear Romeo lumbered toward the couch under framed pictures of Grandma and Grandpa Crumb, over the cheap, imitation Oriental rug, and dodging Mrs. Crumb's trail of used tissues. He saw a tiny light coming from the kitchen. Quickly finding his cozy spot on the sofa Dennis so thoughtfully carved from numerous blankets and pillows, he listened closely to the voices bouncing off the refrigerator door. It was Dennis's parents, and they were arguing about money.

"I just don't know what to do," Mr. Crumb cried, turning on the coffee pot. "How am I supposed to find another job if there aren't any to find?"

"There, there, honey, you need to relax. It's not like you've been fired," Mrs. Crumb consoled. "Besides, maybe Mr. Ward's just had a bad week. You are a wonderful employee, and he knows it."

"Maybe so, but two guys already got their pink slips last week. You should hear what they're going through just to keep it together."

Mrs. Crumb grabbed her husband by the shoulder, bringing him deeper into the kitchen. "Shhh, I don't want Dennis to hear us."

Chapter Thirteeen

"And Dennis, poor Dennis, I know how badly his cat needs that medicine. I don't want Dennis to have to lose him. It'll break his heart, but what can I do? I don't have that kind of money!"

"I know, dear. I know."

Much later after the talking stopped and the tiny light went dim, Romeo finally nodded off to sleep filled with anxiety and worry. He tossed and turned, dreams of Vent City and Alleys pounding in his head. His labored breathing was getting raspier as infection bubbled in his little lungs.

Later still, Romeo awakened with a start to the same tapping at the living room window. He began to feel as though he was living a nightmare. Beat after beat, he covered his ears with a green throw pillow hoping the noises would all go away, but they didn't. The bangs got louder and turned into scratches, until finally he heard a voice. "Romeo, I know you're in there. Open up, this is your father speaking!"

"Could it be?" Romeo wondered. It sure sounded like his father. "But why would he risk coming here?"

Tossing the pillow aside, Romeo carefully poked his head over the armrest of the couch and stared at the window. Behind the sheer, white curtains he could barely make out the creepy silhouette of somebody looking in from the other side. "What if this is a trick?" he whispered to himself. "What if it's

Fidel? Maybe he found out about VC-Day!"

"Romeo, it's Fluffy and your dad! Open the window, we're freezing!"

The voice was familiar.

"What are you guys doing here? It's so late!" Romeo said opening the window with his strongest paw. After Fluffy crawled inside, a second cat poked its head in. "Hey, you're not my dad! Fluffy, what's going on?"

"Trust me, Romeo. I am your father," the other cat claimed. "Fluffy helped me cut and bleach all my fur, even my diamond. I couldn't risk being seen in the city by an Alley, so, I'm in disguise. Listen to my voice! It's really me, son!"

It was his father's voice. Romeo would never forget that voice.

"Get out of that rain. You're all soaked," Romeo said triumphantly in between bouts of coughing as both cats jumped inside.

The three cats sat in silence on the couch, dripping dirty rainwater all over the floor.

"Are you feeling better?" Mr. Gamble finally said. "You don't look so good, son."

"Yeah, Romeo, you look worse than yesterday," Fluffy agreed.

"Thanks!" Romeo snickered. "You don't look so good yourself, Fluffy."

"I'm going to be fine, Romeo," Fluffy reassured. "Just a few bumps and bruises. I'm not sick like you. Now tell us the truth, what'd the doctor say?"

"The truth is, I am sick," Romeo began with a little cough. "The Vet said I need these really expensive pills which Mr. Crumb can't afford to buy. Dennis is very sad. He knows I could die. If that were to happen in front of him, what would I do? I could never come back here! He'd probably think I was a ghost!"

"Don't be silly, Romeo," Mr. Gamble said encouragingly. "We'll figure something out. But first, the plan. There's been some changes. Rumor has it that the Sticks escaped the Factory."

"What?" Romeo asked wide-eyed.

"Yes, it's true. Somehow somebody got a hold of mace, you know, a very painful spray, and maced all the Alleys. The Sticks then ran out of the Factory for their lives while the Alleys became blinded by the stuff."

Romeo grabbed Fluffy by his bows. "That's great!" he cheered. "Then it's all over! And we didn't even have to fight! Dad, I tried to tell you the other day that Fidel's been living at the Factory with his evil gang of Alleys, holding the Sticks hostage. Now that we have the Factory back, you and the other vent guys can come live with us! Together we'll keep the Alleys away forever!"

"It's not going to be that easy, Romeo," his father continued.

"What do you mean?"

"Listen, Fidel still has control of the Factory, and the Alleys are already hunting down your friends," Mr. Gamble explained. "And we have reason to believe that Mr. Sox and Uncle Fred didn't make it out. You can just imagine how angry Fidel must be. We're pretty darn sure he's going to use your friends, Sox and Fred, against us. Maybe even kill them. We've got to act fast, very fast."

"No! Not Mr. Sox!" Romeo cried. "He's a niner!"

"Don't panic, Romeo," Mr. Gamble said, grabbing him by the shoulder. "I have a plan. Rather than waiting until Saturday, we're going in tomorrow. All of us," he reiterated in Fluffy's direction. "We think we can take Fidel and get him out of the Factory without harming Sox and Fred. We've been preparing five years for this, and we're ready for any curves Fidel may throw our way. Knowing where Fidel is only makes our job easier. We go in tomorrow at seven A.M. sharp. You'll have your Factory back, and we'll have our independence. It's time Fidel was taught a lesson once and for all!"

"But dad, I was wondering about something," Romeo sighed.

"What is it?"

"Well, all of those vent animals are so horrible and ugly, no offense, of course. Do you really think they'll be able to walk around the city like any common cat? Won't the people get scared and try to harm them?" Romeo asked.

Mr. Gamble thought for a moment, then sat down. "Good question, son. Yes, that is a concern, but it is one they are willing to take. They know what streets are safe to be on, and who simply can't be seen in the daylight at all. Sort of like what you do already."

"I don't know, dad. I hope it works. Some people can be as cruel as Alleys," Romeo worried.

"We'll cross that bridge when we come to it. Independence, that's our only concern."

"Wow!" Romeo said quickly. "This is so exiting! Tomorrow! We're going to finally get Fidel this time, dad. I feel it. Really, I do. Then we can rebuild the Factory and everything will begin again. You'll see, we can do this together."

"Wait a minute, Romeo," Mr. Gamble broke in. "Yes, all that is possible. A long shot, but possible. Remember, even if you get your Factory back, the Vent City mutants still have a bone to pick with Fidel. He will always have control over us until something much bigger happens."

"Of course, dad, I know that. Once he's out of the Factory, we have to find a way to get rid of him completely!" Romeo made a slashing move across his throat for emphasis. "I'm ready to fight!"

Mr. Gamble swallowed hard looking over at Fluffy for support. "Listen Romeo, I understand how you feel, but you can't fight tomorrow. Look at you! You're barely able to stand up!"

"But father! Fluffy! I've got to help! I've just got to!" Romeo cried, his cough making it harder to persuade them.

"I know you feel responsible, Romeo," Fluffy said. "But you need to sit this one out. You'll die out there. They'll eat you alive. We don't want that to happen. Not like this."

Breaking away from them, Romeo sat at the far side of the couch, his back to their faces. "No, you don't understand! I have to be there! It means everything to me! I don't care if I die!"

"Don't say that, Romeo!" Fluffy pleaded. "If only you had that medicine, maybe you'd be strong enough. But without it..."

"What did you say? If I only had the medicine?" Suddenly, Romeo whipped around, the light bulb above his head hovering steadily. "I've got it! It's so easy. Why don't you two go get the pills for me? I know exactly where the Vet is, and I'm sure you could break in. Get me the medicine and by morning I'll be all better and able to fight! Whadaya say?"

Within moments of getting directions and instructions, Fluffy and Mr. Gamble were off on a miracle.

The entire city was asleep. A few faint, flickering street lamps lit Mr. Gamble and Fluffy's way as violent winds and sharp, sheets of rain sliced through the night. The Sticks' Factory escape had every Alley on the hunt making the streets even more dangerous. Prowling around corners and hiding in shadows, Fluffy and Mr. Gamble would make the ordinarily simple journey to the Vet one of battlefield proportions. Plus Mr. Gamble's silly looking, bleached-white fur made them all the more noticeable. The Alleys may not recognize him as Mr. Gamble, but they'd surely mistake him for a Stick.

Two blocks into their trip, Fluffy had to stop to catch his breath. "I can't run like this, Mr. Gamble," he huffed. "My legs still hurt from the rats."

"We've got to keep going," Mr. Gamble insisted. "There's no time to lose!"

"I'm trying!" Fluffy huffed as he pounded on.

"I see it! I see the building!" Mr. Gamble screamed in front of him. "We're almost there! We can do it! We can do it!"

Through the thick downpour they could see the faint outline of the Vet's building jetting out from all the rest. Having been there before, Fluffy recognized it instantly. He instinctively had that scared, sickening feeling. Their paws pounded hard against the slick pavement, when all of a sudden, a dark shadow rounded the corner ahead of them as if waiting for their arrival. They tried to stop, but hydroplaned as badly as the reckless cab drivers. The spooky, dark form quickly began to take shape as they slid closer and closer. It was Bull and he looked mad. "Turn around, Fluffy!" Mr. Gamble roared. "Go the other way! Bubastis!"

Fluffy did as he was told, but suddenly ran headfirst into another large, grungy dog standing behind him. They were surrounded on either side.

"Well, well, well, what do we have here?" growled Bull, blocking their path with his muscular, canine body. He looked Mr. Gamble up and down with pure disgust. "Are you an Alley? You gots no collar, and no Stick would be *stupid* enough to walk around dis late at night! You're an Alley!"

Mr. Gamble and Fluffy shook from total shock and fear. Bull, his rancid breath nauseating them, walked up smelling them with his flattened nose. His sharp, evil eyes glared into theirs. "What about you?" he growled into Fluffy's face. "You must be a Stick with dat collar and those pathetic bows! What are you? Some sorta pansy or somethin'?"

"Why, I outta...." Fluffy belted forward, quickly shielded by Mr. Gamble.

"Listen, *cats,* I'm missing a Basset, see, and I heard he was killed by a bunch o' cats. I don't suppose you two had anything to do with that, eh?" Bull snarled menacingly.

Mr. Gamble took in a deep breath. "We had nothing to do with that dog's death, got it? *Fidel,* he's your guy. Go find him!"

Chapter Thirteen

"Oh, I plan too, *pussy cat*!" Bull blared eye-to-eye with Mr. Gamble. "But before I do, I think you two need to be taught a lesson. Didn't your mommy ever tell you not to walk around at night in da big, bad city? Hmmm?"

"Get away from us, Bull! We haven't done anything to you!" Mr. Gamble hollered. Suddenly yanking Fluffy by the tail, Gamble bolted across the street zigzagging through the rain as fast as he could. "Come on, Fluffy! Keep running! Keep running!"

"I'm trying!" Fluffy hollered, practically airborne. Bull and his wild bunch charged close behind.

In a flash they were three blocks away, the sound of Bull's howls closing in. Vaulting over benches, garbage, and bums, the two cats found themselves running farther from their destination and into the creepier depths of the city. Just when the howling and barking seemed far enough away, Mr. Gamble ducked behind a banged up dumpster, panting heavily. "I...I think we've...lost them. Let's go back...we've got to go...back."

"I can't! I can't do it!" Fluffy coughed. "We're too far. Bull will get us for sure. If he doesn't, the Alleys definitely will!"

"Look, I'm going back to that Vet for Romeo!" Mr. Gamble protested, slowly gaining his breath back. "Either you can give up or you can come with me. Now, what's your choice going to be?"

Chapter Thirteen

Without a word, Fluffy stood up and nodded. Of course, he was going back.

Like before, the two cats dashed through the city, this time even more cautiously than before. Trudging to outwit Bull and his vicious pack, they took the long way, walking far uptown, then back downtown again to avoid crossing their path. Their cat eyes darted everywhere for hiding Alleys ready to attack. There was only one Bull, but dozens of Alleys.

After a long and scary run, they made it back to the Vet. Shivering and tired, they took a moment to catch their breath underneath the dry entryway. Above the awning Mr. Gamble quickly spotted an open window on the third floor. To their advantage it was directly beside a tall telephone pole with convenient stepping rods. Once inside, Fluffy led Mr. Gamble straight to the Vet's office behind a large, brown door.

"How will we get in? The door's locked!" Mr. Gamble asked, his words echoing down the long hallway.

Snooping around, Fluffy found the perfect solution. "Here, Mr. Gamble! Through this mail slot!"

Sure enough, Fluffy had found a small opening for mail just above the doorknob. Tight though it was, it provided just enough space for the two of them to crawl through.

"There you go, Mr. Gamble," Fluffy struggled, hoisting Romeo's father up and over his head and into the slot.

Fluffy heard Mr. Gamble fall with a thump on the other side of the door. Taking a running leap, Fluffy jumped at the opening. He hung by his claws and hoisted himself up. Every time he wiggled his bottom higher into the slot, the harder the little gold flapping mail door would slap him. Considering how much his body hurt to begin with, he certainly didn't like it.

Inside the empty waiting room instantly brought back unwelcomed shivers for Fluffy. He hadn't been there since the *operation,* but those memories were so vivid and stinging, just the antiseptic smell alone nearly sent him into convulsions. For a moment he stood staring at the row of orange, plastic chairs and twitched like a broken toy. Mr. Gamble grabbed him by the collar to break his trance.

"Pills? I believe Romeo said they'd be behind the main desk, right Fluffy?" Mr. Gamble asked, snickering at his reflection in a large, metal water bowl.

"Uh, yeah...that's it. The desk. The desk. The desk," Fluffy said robotically, imagining the horrors of the dreaded thermometer.

"Come on, snap out of it!" Mr. Gamble warned. "Let's get this over with. Tomorrow's a big day, and I'm going to need some rest. Besides, this place gives me the creeps."

"You can say that again," Fluffy moaned, struck by a sudden pinching tummy ache. Fluffy saw the rows and rows of charts and records, his own dusty file being in there somewhere. *Four pound, white male feline,* he remembered the doctor saying, scribbling away. The files stood precariously on shaky-looking metal shelves along the back wall behind the main desk. As a coding device, different colored stickers set one file apart from another, red for cat, blue for dog, the green he didn't know. Then Fluffy remembered. One afternoon as he, Romeo, and Snickers were out playing, he spotted one of those folders with a green sticker laying in the gutter. Always nosey, they scoured through the soggy papers and melted x-rays. It was just around the time they were all learning how to read. The words were just blurry ink splotches, but Fluffy was able to make out one for sure. *Monkey*. "Monkey," he remembered saying. "Who would ever want a monkey?"

"I found them! I found them!" Mr. Gamble hollered deep inside somewhere. "I found Romeo's pills! Yep, they're his alright! I can read his name and everything!"

"Well, that was easy. Mr. Gamble, where are you anyway?" Fluffy asked, searching the drawers behind the desk, finding lots of rubber bands and doggie bones. "I don't see you!"

"I'm over here! In the cabinet behind you!"

Sure enough, it was Mr. Gamble's silly looking neon fur that gave him away. Once Fluffy looked up and over the desk, he could plainly see Mr. Gamble glowing from behind the clear, plastic cabinet door like a beacon. Suddenly, the door slammed shut, suctioning against its strong magnetic strip. Mr. Gamble pounded frantically from the other side. Immediately recognizing his predicament, Fluffy jumped up to the top of the desk and stretched his paw to the cabinet door. After three hearty tugs, it opened. Mr. Gamble popped out, panting dramatically as if he were in there for days.

"Thanks, Fluffy. That was scary! My whole life flashed before my eyes." Mr. Gamble found himself in plain view of the three examining rooms that lay to his right passed another swinging door. Through the door's large, circular window he was able to see several Pound-like metal cages inside holding different animals. "Wow, poor guys," he said plainly, not noticing Fluffy's expression.

Looking through that round window at all the sad, lonely faces on the other side, Fluffy started to cry. It wasn't just the sweet, little kitty faces. Not just the ones covered in bandages or stabbed with needles or those awful lampshade collars. It wasn't the whimpering dogs, or the rabbit with his long, jagged scar. It was all of them, all of them combined that got to him. Seeing them squashed into those cramped spaces made him realize how bonded these animals actually were. Once he saw their watery eyes peeking through the cage bars, it didn't matter who was cat or dog or rabbit for that matter, for they all shared the same familiar look of fear. For just a moment, a brief moment, he pitied them equally. "I should let them go," he whispered low, the animals scratching at the bars and whimpering to him for help.

Being the adult, Mr. Gamble gently nudged Fluffy. "This isn't the Pound," he said with compassion. "These animals are being helped. Don't take them away from their families when they're sick. They won't survive out there alone in their weakened conditions. This is the best place for them now, even if they don't know it just yet. Come on, son. Let's go."

With the bottle of pills tucked tightly under Fluffy's collar, the two cats slipped back through the mail slot and headed for the third floor window. Back in the Vet's hospital ward, Mr. Shadow slept quietly and comfortably in his newspaper lined cage. If Fluffy had looked a little lower, he would have seen his dear old friend and teacher.

Chapter Fourteen

Fluffy and Mr. Gamble scampered down the telephone pole to the sidewalk. The pills still intact, Fluffy crept around the corner looking for any unforeseen trouble that may lay ahead. Carefully sticking his neck out, he was able to see all the way down the shadowy streets to where they disappeared. The rain had stopped leaving a wispy, grey fog hovering near the ground. For such a big city, it was awfully quiet out there.

"The coast is clear!" he called back to Mr. Gamble. "Let's go!"

"I'll feel much better once Romeo takes his pills, and I get back to Vent City. I have a lot of last minute stuff to do before tomorrow's invasion. But first I'll..."

Suddenly, Mr. Gamble was cut off by a loud, screeching meow.

Chapter Fourteen

"What was that? Who's out there?" Mr. Gamble said cautiously, shielding young Fluffy behind his back, his eyes darting left to right.

"Hissss!!" they heard again, followed by the ghastly sight of three wrathful Alleys charging their way, nostrils flaring.

"Run, Fluffy! Run!" Mr. Gamble shouted. But it was too late! The Alleys had them cornered. Beet red Alley eyes and razor sharp fangs glistened through the fog. Their matted, greasy fur hung like cheap, thrift store suits.

"Well, well, well! What do we have here?" said one of the Alleys.

"Which one do I get, huh?" the littlest and smelliest of the three asked, slobbering all over himself in the process.

Boil, the biggest Alley, ran his long tongue across the sharp edges of his teeth. "Boy, won't Fidel be proud of us? Two of 'em! I bet none of the others will get two of 'em!"

Fluffy and Mr. Gamble shook their heads in disbelief, their paws rattling in the puddle beneath them. "Wait, fellas, you've got it all wrong," Mr. Gamble began hesitantly. "We're not the guys you're looking for. We're not the Stick escapees."

"Yeah, were no Sticks," Fluffy said with a nervous, phony laugh. "In fact, I thoughts I seen some over der," he pointed down the moon speckled street.

"If you're no Stick, then why's you got dat collar on?" Boil cleverly asked.

"Yeah, and what's wit the bottle? You some sorta druggy?" the smelly one teased.

With the three leery Alleys surrounding them, Mr. Gamble and Fluffy turned to each other, yelling simultaneously, "Run! Run!"

Like bandits, they burst through the Alleys, charging down the sidewalk as fast as their paws could carry them. Fluffy pounded on with all the strength he could muster, thinking only of Romeo and the pills. For Mr. Gamble, a deep crack in the sidewalk appeared out of nowhere trapping his paw as Fluffy zoomed by. Mr. Gamble's body flung forward sending him crashing down with a horrible, splashing thud. He let out a final scream which echoed in Fluffy's ears. Fluffy instantly turned to see Mr. Gamble laying helpless, his twisted paw holding him down against the concrete.

"Get up! Let's go!" Fluffy hollered, seeing the Alleys charging closer. But there was no time. All at once the Alleys heaved forward pouncing on poor Mr. Gamble. He fought and struggled to get them off, but it was no use. All three of them had pinned him down, his head smashed into a dirty puddle. Fluffy knew there was nothing he could do for him now. Mr. Gamble was caught and would be taken to Fidel. While the Alleys tackled Mr. Gamble, Fluffy seized the moment and ran.

Chapter Fourteen

"Get him, Buck! The other one's getting away!" one Alley roared, looking up.

Fluffy glanced back and saw the little Alley jump up and run straight for him with pure evil in his eyes. For just a second, Mr. Gamble lifted his head and with all his lungpower shouted, "Go!"

Saving himself, Fluffy burst forward, the little Alley hot on his tail. Knowing the streets as well as any Alley, Fluffy soon saw a hiding spot Mr. Shadow had showed them during survival class. It was a small space between two large cement blocks. Using his sideways fake-em-out technique, he quickly ducked into the crevice, the Alley cat flying right passed him. Breathing a heavy sigh of relief, Fluffy glanced down at his sweaty body, immediately noticing something wrong. Romeo's pills! The bottle was open! Instantly, he reached down clutching the broken bottle between his front paws. Like he suspected, many of the pills were gone, splattered all over the wet, treacherous streets. It would be too risky to try and find the tablets. Besides, the rainwater had most likely dissolved them. Luckily for Romeo, six little pills remained at the bottom of the plastic bottle which only moments early held thirty-six. Like a snake, Fluffy snuck out of his hiding place and slithered back to Romeo's home.

Romeo heard Fluffy's knock at the window and carefully helped him inside. It was immediately obvious to Romeo that something had gone awry.

Fluffy's eyes gave it away

"What happened, Fluffy? Tell me what happened?" Romeo looked down, his eyes finding the bottle. "Where's my father?"

"Look, Romeo, the Alleys got him. We outwitted Bull, even found the pills," he huffed, holding up the bottle, "but the Alleys found us. They got your dad. I couldn't do anything about it! I'm sorry, Romeo, but they were going to get me too. I couldn't do that to you. You need these." He spilled the remaining six pills on the coffee table for Romeo to see.

"Oh, God! Not my dad!" Romeo cried. "It's my fault for making you get my medicine!"

"Don't be silly, Romeo."

"I can't believe this. I just can't believe it." Sadly, Romeo picked up two of the pills with his mouth and sucked them down at his water bowl. In the kitchen, he leaned against the humming refrigerator feeling its coolness on his feverish body. "What about tomorrow? What's going to happen now?"

Fluffy leapt off the couch and joined Romeo in the kitchen. "I don't know. What can any of us do without your father?" It was then that a sudden and daring plan sprang to Romeo's mind. He stared hypnotically at Fluffy.

"No way, Romeo. I know what you're thinking, and it's not going to work," Fluffy said, reading his thoughts. "Besides, you're too sick!"

"But it's perfect! The perfect plan!" Romeo paced around the kitchen stomping over Pierre's messy food. "Fluffy, I've got to go down to Vent City tomorrow and help those animals for my father! I'll take over! Let's do it, Fluffy! Come with me!"

"Hey, leave me outta this! I don't know your plan anyway!"

"But you know the Factory! Besides, don't you want to be there?" Romeo exploded.

"That was when your dad was going to be there too," Fluffy added. "Without him there..."

Romeo held Fluffy tightly by the shoulders. "Think of Mr. Sox and Uncle Fred, and my dad! Don't you want to be there when we face up to Fidel? We can do it, Fluff! We're ready!"

A million thoughts raced through Romeo's mind. Could he really do this? Could he actually take his father's place? "Fluffy, I need your answer. Are you with me?"

With his paw on Romeo, Fluffy said confidently, "I'll go with you, buddy. You know I will. We can lead them together. It's time."

"Attaboy, Fluffy. You won't regret it. Now, find Darla in the morning. See if MayBelle and Calvin will come too. We need all the help we can get."

"Look out Alleys, we're coming back!" Fluffy shouted, slipping out of the window. "Yeah-hoo!!"

As Romeo waited for the pills to take effect, he paced back and forth along the deep couch cushions trying desperately to remember all his father taught him about the invasion. He would think about it all night long.

Early in the morning and with not much sleep, Romeo awoke feeling less achy. The pills were working. Dennis noticed right away. It was nice to see him smile again.

After Mr. Crumb ambled off to work, Romeo crept into Dennis's room. In his mouth were the four remaining pills. He swallowed two more, and when nobody was looking hid the other two behind Dennis's desk. Dennis would never notice. He never sat at that old desk anyway. Besides, he was too busy getting ready for school.

If Dennis didn't find his science book, he'd be late for school again. He didn't know what was worse, being late or being caught without his science book. His teacher hated it when the students left things at home. "Excuses," she often said, "are for the weak." Tearing his room apart, Dennis searched on. He'd be the laughing stock of the class, not just for losing a book, but for losing the fourth book this year.

"Dennis! You'll be late for school! Get off your butt and get going!" his mother howled from the living room, refluffing the cushions Romeo smushed.

"Alright, alright." Without even a goodbye

wink, Dennis ran off. Romeo jumped up on the desk and waited the usual forty-two seconds it took Dennis to dash down the stairs and burst onto the sidewalk below. Romeo liked looking out the window as his eyes followed Dennis's floppy hair and awkward body bounce off to school.

Knowing what an important day he had in front of him, Romeo decided to fill his empty belly with whatever gruel awaited him.

"Where do you zink you're going?" Pierre mumbled, gnawing on Dennis's missing science book.

"What's it to you?" Romeo asked.

Spitting out a page on meteors, Pierre continued. "It doesn't matter to *moi*, but I wouldn't go out if I were you." Snobbishly, he leaned against the wall biting at his puppy nails.

"Why? What are you talking about, Pierre?"

"Well, let's just say...I heard a little story zat some of the Sticks escaped and the Alleys are *tres* mad," Pierre related.

Romeo stepped on a passing ant as he began to walk away. "I know that. I know all about that. But I don't..."

"And they say Fidel's expecting you."

Suddenly Romeo stopped. "What did you say?" he asked quickly. "Pierre, what did you mean by that?"

"Oh, nothing for you to worry about, *mon*

precious *petit* Romeo," Pierre mumbled, his wet nose to the air.

"Look, you'd better stop playing games with me! Now, if there's something I gotta know, spit it out! You hear me? Spit it out!" He raced up to Pierre and for the first time grabbed him by the collar. "Spill it, Frenchie!"

Pierre broke down his tough facade and whined like a puppy. "Alright! Alright! Just let go of my collar, *s'il vous plait*!"

Romeo released his grip throwing Pierre back to the floor. "Zat's all I know. I swear! Some of the other dogs were talking about how the Sticks escaped, and Fidel is figuring you'll show your little self sooner or later. I swear, zat's all I know!" Pierre coughed his throat back into shape.

"Well, I'm going. They need me out there," Romeo said proudly.

"Why would they need *vous?* You're just a *petit* kitty," Pierre argued.

"What do you know anyway? You're just a dog," he said knowing full well that Pierre was probably right. What *was* he getting himself into?

Later that day Romeo found himself in front of an angry mass of mutants deep below the streets in Vent City. It was particularly dark down there for such an anticipated day. Cobwebs danced in the smelly breeze and a wicked gurgle bubbled near

Chapter Fourteen

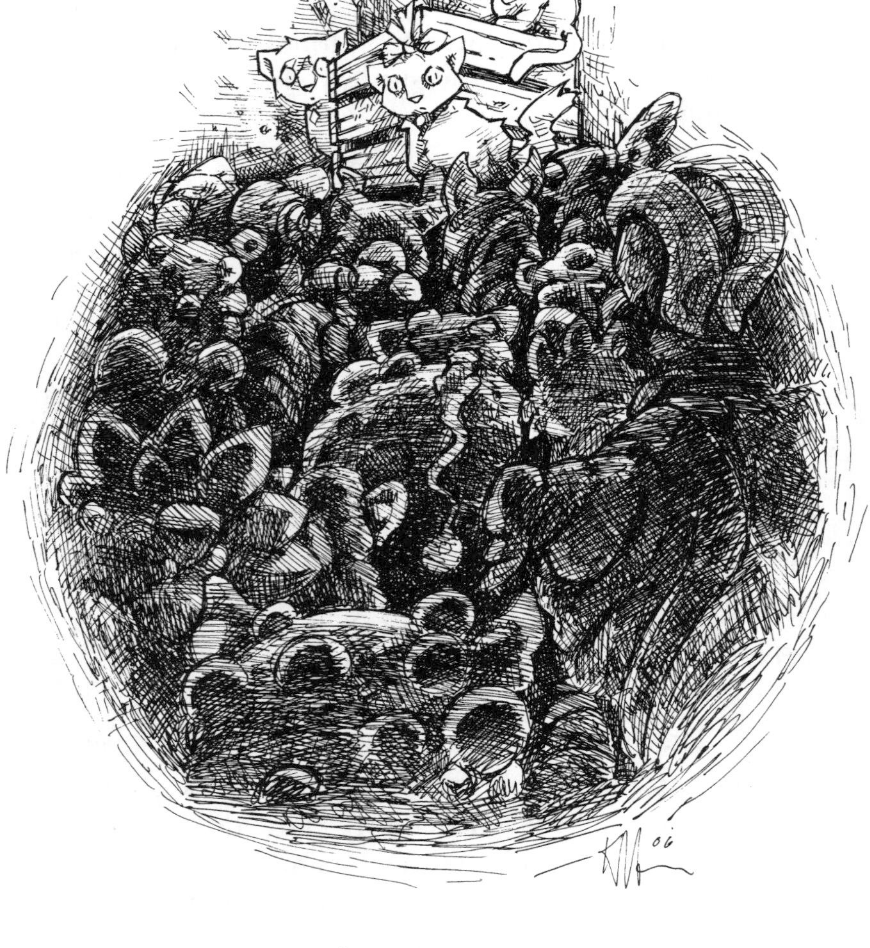

the river. Romeo sat nervously behind a splintered, wooden crate. Left over from the original subway construction, it served as the next best thing to a podium. Next to Romeo stood Fluffy. Behind them was Darla. She made it. Not Calvin though, he was too busy being photographed by every newspaper and magazine in town. Nothing could tear him away from that kind of glorified attention, not even this. As for Tabitha, she was still too shaken to even consider leaving her home. For Romeo, his second dose of medicine was serving him well.

At the front of the crowd, Bradley, Mr. Gamble's assistant, desperately explained what happened to Mr. Gamble and the situation at hand much to everyone's dismay.

"Whadaya mean Mr. G's not comin'?" a disturbing bird-like thing called from the back.

"What the heck are we supposed to do now?" someone shouted. "What about all our plans? What about the invasion? We've been ready to go since seven this morning? I knew those guys'd be trouble! I just knew it!"

"Yeah!" stormed the group, pounding and cursing the air. "What's going to happen to us?"

"Romeo and Fluffy are here to help!" Bradley yelled.

"We want Mr. G!" somebody demanded.

Watching tensely behind the makeshift podium, Romeo and Fluffy shivered as the crowd bellowed out of control. They grew louder and louder, throwing the smaller animals into the air and shaking the ground beneath them.

"Listen, folks, listen," Fluffy hollered as a flying two week old rotten tomato splattered all over his face. Scraping off the gooey mess, he continued. "Can I please have your attention?" Another tomato sailed by, this one bigger than the last. "You *must* listen to us! This is important! Don't you understand?"

"Let me try," Romeo suggested.

"It's no use, Romeo," Fluffy wallowed. "They just won't listen. Don't put yourself through this Romeo, it's..."

"Excuse me, excuse me, everybody," Romeo shouted. "I'm Mr. Gamble's son, Romeo, and these are my friends! We've come here today to help you!"

"Are we fighting today or not?" the tomato launcher screamed, new ammunition ready to burn.

"How do we know we can trust these guys?" Hayward blurted out.

"Yeah, what if it's a trick?" stormed Ebenezer, a rat. He was so vile to look at, the cats wouldn't dare eat him, and the rat colony had abandoned him as one of their own.

"But they're our only option! They know the city! We haven't been out in years! They've promised to help us and they have as much reason to fight as we do!" Wanda rallied on.

"He's right! Today is your day!" Romeo roared with a sudden burst of grown-up authority. "Today is the day we will finally see justice!"

Wanting some of the glory, Fluffy retook the stand. "Let's join together and conquer that monster once and for all! Rid this city of him!" From the back another tomato hurled for his head.

"I don't understand this," Romeo whispered to Fluffy. "They don't seem to want to listen to you."

Fluffy grimaced and pouted and pretended not to be bothered by the annoying tomato seeds stuck deep in his ears. "Well, just go ahead and take over, *Mr. Romeo*! Just like on the island! See if I care!"

"Awe come on, Fluffy, lighten up," Romeo whined. "They just associate me with my dad!"

"Whatever," Fluffy mumbled, slumping on the ground.

All of a sudden, nearly every mutant began to chant, "Rom-e-o! Rom-e-o! Rom-e-o!" They jumped up and down with enthusiasm, passion, and zeal. The few skeptics stood motionless and silent. Snubbing Romeo with a snarling glare, Fluffy joined Darla far behind the podium. His wounded feelings left him wondering if he should even bother to stay. Seeing all the eager faces in the crowd looking toward Romeo for answers, he knew he had to buckle down and cooperate no matter how insignificant he became.

After one final meeting, the invasion was set and ready. They'd strike the Factory as planned.

Chapter Fourteen

But first each and every mutant, regardless of their handicap, was checked and rechecked for physical and emotional readiness, and quizzed on their knowledge of the attack. If and when a mutant passed this final inspection, it was immediately released to base, a small area near the murky river where everyone was told to wait for the others.

"Name," Wanda asked the next mutant in line.

"Squash," he replied. Squash was originally a cat but with such a horribly deformed and warped head. He now actually resembled a summer squash. Unfortunately, he smelled like a rotted one. Wanda, not such a beauty herself, had a hard time standing near him.

"Position please," Wanda asked him, casually staring at the ground.

"I'm on the first scare team," Squash answered proudly.

"Task?"

"To startle the Alleys with my repulsive looks, sir."

"Uh, *ma'am* will be fine," Wanda said.

"Sorry."

"Purpose?"

"To scare the Alleys, allowing the first fight team to enter successfully, ma'am," Squash continued.

"Good. Now, what if they scare you first? The Alleys, I mean," she asked.

"Won't happen, ma'am. I'm ready. I've been

waiting for this for a long time. I can just see those Alleys screaming and running for their lives! I've dreamed it! I have! I'm going to give them something to see they'll never forget!" he proclaimed, fist raised high in the air.

"Good."

After each and every mutant was checked, the time had finally come.

"Let's go out there today and do some serious damage!" Romeo hollered above the crowd, Fluffy snickering behind him. "Together we can fight against the evil forces that have plagued our lives for so long! For me, the Alleys killed my mother and brothers, have taken my father and your leader captive, tortured my friends and made the city a danger zone for years! They have robbed you of your freedom and well, let's face it, your looks! Now get out there and fight for our rights!"

"Hurray!" they all shouted with heightened excitement.

"Yeah, let's do it!" Fluffy cheered, as yet another tomato sailed his way.

"What about the female? The Alley female?" George snapped. "She's our lure."

"Uh, we'll use her later. Let's go!" Romeo roared, knowing full well he had no intention of using Candle at all. But he didn't know why.

Romeo charged forward leading everyone up the cold, rusted TV ladder as they headed straight for the vent. The mighty herd followed closely behind, seething and drooling angry blobs of foam. Chester was strongly secured to his safety scooter.

Up they all went, higher and higher over the stacks of cracked TVs and broken antennas. The place was dripping in old spider webs and oozing in sewer slime. Almost near the top, Romeo turned to see the dozens of motley followers climbing toward their destiny. At the bottom of the mound, Fluffy and Darla brought up the rear.

"We're almost there!" Bradley exclaimed as he flapped his wings. "Keep coming! Keep coming!"

Up ahead, Romeo could see the faint hint of light coming from the escape vent when he felt a cold chill run up his back. Again and again the strange breeze seemed to wrap around him, zooming all over the place making strange, spooky noises.

"Oh my! It's...it's Fernando the truck driver! He's back! He's going to ruin everything!" Wanda shouted three TVs behind.

"Who? Who is Fernando?" Romeo hollered, feeling the crisp wind zigzag around him.

Bradley dashed up the ladder grabbing hold of Romeo. "Fernando! The truck driver who died driving the toxic waste truck! He comes back every year to get us! Run! Run for your lives!"

The climbing mutants began to frantically swarm around each other, falling and dangling out of control.

"I don't understand!" Romeo shouted above the cries. "Why is he mad at you guys? Why doesn't he find the Alleys?"

"He's just mad! Don't you see? He's a ghost! He doesn't know who killed him! He's just mad! Now what are you going to do, Romeo *Gamble*? How are you going to get us out of here?" Bradley exploded.

Standing atop the mountain of rubbish, Romeo watched horrified as the mutants crashed back and forth, fleeing from Fernando's ghostly wrath. "Keep climbing!" he wailed. "There's no such thing as ghosts!"

Wrong! Suddenly Romeo came face to face with the angry ghost, his yellow eyes piercing the darkness. Still in his grey trucker's uniform, he howled and moaned through his long, rough beard, his heavy, massive body ready for revenge. Some of the mutants struggled on, while others tumbled down to the bottom, lost forever in the murky river.

"Never mind them! We've got to keep going!" Bradley squealed.

Up, up, up they climbed despite the haunting, ghostly attempts to keep knocking them down forever. Below, Fluffy and Darla shut their eyes tightly and lunged forward, their pounding hearts and rushing blood pushing them upwards.

Just when their fears reached an all time high, dozens of mammoth, nasty rats appeared out of nowhere, screeching and shrilling at the top of the TVs.

"Oh, no!" Romeo howled, staring right into their beady, red eyes. "Not them too!"

But instead of creating another roadblock, the evil rats, presumably out to destroy the mutants as was so often their purpose, suddenly leapt forward completely devouring Fernando's swirling ghost. Like voracious maggots, they entirely covered him allowing the mutants just enough time to reach the vent.

"Onward!" Romeo charged.

In a rush they all pushed forward heading for the waiting vent. Fluffy, being the last, looked behind one more time to see three sad, little animals coughing and choking their way down the river as Fernando and the huge rats tangled in the wicked current.

In no time Romeo lifted the vent. Certain there was no train coming down the tracks, he shoved each and every mutant into the station. "Go! Go! Go!" he hollered, holding the wire cover open.

"This is it guys!" someone cried out excitedly.

The mutants raced out and across the tracks. One by one they charged on just as a train stormed into the station.

"A train! A train!" Romeo yelled. "Hurry!"

"Go, Romeo! I'll hold the vent!" Bradley insisted. "They need you up there! You know where to go!"

"Alright!" Romeo agreed, just as Fluffy and Darla pierced through the vent ahead of him. "Hurry up, Bradley! Don't get left behind!"

The ground rumbled and rolled as the morning train quickly zoomed into the station. Most mutants waited dazed and confused on the platform, but several of them still stood frozen on the dangerous tracks. "Come on!" others shouted. "Get off the tracks! Get off the tracks!"

However, the shock and bewilderment of the moment caught them off guard. Just as their minds snapped into place, the massive train roared through the station hitting their bodies. In that split second Romeo and the others caught the horrified faces of the mutants as they realized their doom. They now lay crushed beneath the train.

"We must move forward!" Romeo cried, clinging tightly to his fleeting hope. "We can't stop now!" He was their leader, and he had to be tough. He had to do what he had to do, like it or not.

"No! No!" cried one disfigured squirrel as she teetered dangerously near the platform's edge. "Johnny? Johnny, are you down there?"

Just then, the human subway patrons noticed the infestation of ghastly creatures before them. "Oh my God!" cried the engineer. "Call the police!" Screaming and pushing each other aside, the commuters shoved their way onto the train, grabbing their children and hiding behind the seats.

Chapter Fourteen

As the train pushed away, Romeo and the others saw the horrifying sight of their dead friends splattered on the tracks, Squash and his funny, little head being one of them. He now looked like squash pie.

"He's gone! He's gone! My Johnny's gone!" the squirrel wailed as she stared at the grisly sight below.

"There's no time to stop! Keep moving!" Bradley yelled desperately from the other side of the tracks.

Romeo, sickened by the entire fiasco, led everyone outside the station. Once into the crisp and cloudy day, the mutants felt the cold air run through their fur for the first time in years. Scores of buildings and cars and city noises took their hearts by surprise leaving them standing in awe and wonderment in spite of the pent up pain and anger that still ravaged inside them. What a sight to see. Nobody cared if it was raining. Nobody cared about the dirty taxis and broken down stores. Nobody cared about the littered gutters and the disinterested people. They were outside! Part of the world! Not stuck under a vent with no light, no air, no life. Fidel and his lot took all this away from them, and they weren't going to accept it for one more lousy minute! They were part of the world again, and they were there to stay!

"On to the Factory!" Romeo shouted.

And they all followed.

Chapter Fifteen

As Romeo and the mutants tore through the city, more and more havoc followed as the stunned people met this weird army. Like in the subway station, the surprised humans flew out of the way of the nasty beasts, women screaming, children crying. They zoomed down the dreary city streets, pushing themselves faster and faster. Without a wince, the sewer gang ran on, unaware they had stirred every mind in the city to a point of near delirium.

"We're under attack!" one panicked shopkeeper yelled. "The city is under siege!"

"Run inside! Run for your lives! Aliens are attacking!" a cop screamed, zigzagging through the honking cars.

Romeo and the others pounded on toward their destination, charging down the streets. And up ahead, the Factory! Standing like a lonely, forgotten castle, it waited under the endless grey sky. "There it is!" Romeo called. "It's that dilapidated building on the left! First scare team, follow me!"

In a cloud of dust the Vent City mutants reached the Factory. "Let's go!" shouted Bradley. "Charge!"

Romeo and the rest of the first scare team crawled through the Factory door. Winding their way down the long, empty hallways of sleeping candles, Romeo silenced the crowd as they tiptoed to the rec room door.

"Shhh, Fidel's in there," Romeo whispered, looking over at his team. Designed to startle the Alleys, this team from Vent City was the ugliest and most mutated of them all. They were inside-out, covered in puss-filled scabs, dripping in gooey slime, and drooling a heavy, putrid slop. Even Romeo still gagged at the sight of them. Still, they looked to him for their next move. They were counting on him. He could not let them down. Glancing at a torn drawing of Bubastis for strength, Romeo took a deep breath and faced the door. "On the count of three we go. One, two, three..."

Like wasps, they exploded through the wooden door zipping into the rec room. Rummaging throughout, shrieking and wailing in their moment of power, they overturned every pillow and chair. But something was wrong. Very wrong. The cold room was silent and deserted.

"Where are all the Alleys? Where is Fidel?" Myrna screamed, breathing heavier than she ever had before.

"They're probably upstairs in the library," Romeo said loudly. "Follow me through the other door! I know the way!"

However just as Romeo turned around, the rec room door slammed shut locking him in along with the mutants. An eerie silence encompassed them in a heavy coat of incredible tension and suspense. Romeo's eyes darted everywhere. Then slowly and carefully, they all gravitated toward the center of the room. Together, they clung to each other shaking in the thick darkness.

Suddenly the far door flung open and a bubbling throng of Alleys whirled in, hollering like evil itself. Instantly the Alleys ominously surrounded the Vent City mutants. In the center of it all was Romeo, grumbling at the cruelty around them. Pierre was right. The Alleys were waiting for him. "Attack!" Romeo suddenly yelled.

The mutants charged, viciously grappling at the Alleys as they pushed forward, but they were no match for the stronger cats. Though the first scare team was ugly and intimidating, they lacked strength and proportioned bodies necessary to fight very long. Their slimy skin and drooping eyes were no match. The Alleys were having a field day. All of a sudden, a loud banging came from the other side of the door. Everyone looked. Just in the nick of time, it was the first fight team of mutants pounding on the Factory walls and boarded up windows. "Let us in!" Fluffy roared from outside. "Fidel! Let us in and fight like cats!"

But it was no use. The harder the mutants pounded to get in, the louder and more fierce the Alleys fought the scare team. "Pathetic! Dat's what you guys are! Pathetic!" echoed Max's deep, belligerent voice as he pummeled an inside-out creature.

"Why are dey so ugly?" Bait roared. "Who are deese weirdoes?"

"Shut up, Bait! Just keep fightin'!" Max shouted back. "Turn your head if you have to!"

As the Alleys were about to finally rid the world of Romeo and the scare team, Fluffy and the fight team erupted through a secret back window unknown to the Alleys. Covered in dirt, Fluffy and his winded followers devilishly ran around like ferocious maniacs, outnumbering the Alleys four to one.

Across the cold battlefield, attack after brutal attack ensued, blood splattering, furballs flying, curdling screams echoing. Mass destruction. At this point, it was too difficult to see who was winning and who was losing. Romeo himself took on two raving Alleys, each bigger and fiercer than he. They tossed him around like a rag doll, his bodily aches threefold. Still, he fought on overcome by rage and the celestial purple glow that pierced through a cracked beam in the corner.

"Get outta here! Dis is our territory now!" screeched Bait as he viciously tore at Fluffy's blue ribbons.

"Never!" Fluffy snapped back. "Never!"

"Take *dis*!" Cheeseburger growled, swinging Chester, the boneless dog, around in circles purposely smacking him into the high wooden beams like an old dishrag.

"Helfht! Helfth!" Chester cried, unsuccessfully attempting to kick Cheeseburger in the head.

"Get away from him or you'll be sorry!" Romeo warned.

But Cheeseburger kept right on whipping Chester in circles, laughing like a hyena the whole time.

"You guys are so ugly!" Steak hollered at the top of his Alley lungs.

"I can't take this anymore!" cried Hayward, the eyeballed squirrel. "I've got to get out of here! Get me out of here! Get me out of here!"

"Get a hold of yourself!" Romeo shouted from across the room as the Alleys moved in closer and closer, taunting the mutants with their deadly scowls. As fast as he could, Hayward suddenly darted for the door, recklessly stumbling through the Alleys. Others followed.

"Help! Help!" the sewer pack screamed,

charging for the exit.

"Come back!" Romeo howled. "They'll kill you out there! We've got to stick together and fight here and now!"

It was too late. Several others raced like fiends through the door.

"Nooo!" wailed Romeo. "Stop! I demand you stop!"

A group of Alleys rushed after them, violently plunging their pointy claws into the escapees' mangled flesh, slicing them to shreds.

A lucky few managed to flee, only to be met by the scores of Alleys surrounding the Factory camouflaged high in the trees and the dirt mounds. The concealed Alleys leapt from their clever hiding spots trampling any non-Alley in their way. Some mutants managed to bolt through the menacing wrath, high tailing it onto the busy city streets. They helplessly ran between the panicked people searching desperately for a way back to the safety of the familiar vents.

The fighting continued in the bushes, on the sidewalks, wherever possible. At one point, three Alleys came flying down from the tallest tree landing on top of two boneless cats. "Ah-ha! Flattened you!" one of the Alleys cackled.

"You didn't flatten us!" one boneless bravely cried out. "We're already flat, you idiot!"

Then, all of the boneless banded together,

wrapping themselves tightly around an Alley like the skin on a new basketball. With the Alley trapped inside of them, they rolled and rolled down the street, the cat screaming from under their squishy flesh. Seeing a high gutter swirling before them, the boneless tumbled with full force. They released their grip just as the Alley smashed against the hard concrete like a bowling ball and fell into the sewer.

"Gotcha!" one of the mutants snapped back, dizzy and faint.

Dozens of Alleys fought off the remainder of the repulsive creatures. Each vent member fought with every bit of energy he had left, biting the vicious Alleys who clawed at and clung to their bodies, dodging deadly swats that sliced through their flesh. The Alleys were beyond brutal.

Back inside the Factory, Romeo and the remaining soldiers gallantly fought against the impossible. Victory seemed inconceivable. Suddenly, Romeo was slung to the ground by an angry swipe. Laying winded and breathless on the floor, he found Bait looming over him, a ruthless grimace slapped across his comical face.

"Well, well, well," Bait snarled patronizingly, "who do we have here? If it ain't *Romeo*, my favorite Stick. What brings you here, eh?"

"Where are my...Stick friends? What have you done with them?" Romeo begged shamelessly.

"Oh, no need to worry about dem, little fella.

Fidel's got dem all nice and cozy like," he growled with a rotten giggle, rubbing his blood stained paws together like sand paper. "Don't fret your little, pink nose for a minute."

"Why I outta..," Romeo lunged, ready and raring to fight on. Then he heard a terrible cry from behind a chair.

"No! Stop!" screamed an odd two-headed cat, both its heads being pushed together like a peanut butter sandwich.

"Take that!" rang Steak, helping his buddy Fish finish the job.

The mutant tumbled to the ground in misery, its two noses suctioned together.

By now the battle in the Factory escalated to barbaric proportions.

"Look out beee-low!" one Alley hollered from atop the highest beam in the room. With a devilish laugh he flung a large slab of wood to the ground painfully crushing three other mutants, including Wanda.

"Help, Romeo! Help!" Wanda shouted, her roach legs stuck under the plank.

Immediately upon hearing her scream, Romeo dashed to save her. Shoving Bait out of his way hard, he shouted, "Grab my paw! Quick!"

Romeo pulled her out as the other two mutants involved struggled to get free from beneath the beam as well. Seeing their little paws and ears sticking out,

Romeo instantly called for Fluffy. Together they lifted the wood, saving the crushed mutants from certain death. Though Wanda was unhurt, the other two were not so lucky. Their legs were broken, their tails crushed. Like wounded soldiers, they writhed on the floor in throbbing pain.

"Romeo! Over here!" Darla shrieked now pinned to the ground on her stomach, Bait sitting heavily on her back with his entire, ratty body.

"How do you like that, sweetie?" he taunted, bending Darla's leg backwards.

"Ouch!" Darla squealed. "Get offa me!"

Taking in a deep breath, Romeo jumped as high as he could, soaring over three other Alleys. He landed firmly on Bait's head. With a wail, Bait flung to the ground as he and Romeo rolled all over the floor, clawing each other to the bone.

"Let's see how *you* like it!" Romeo cried, digging his nails deeply into Bait's lanky body.

Before they knew it, they were wrestling themselves to the far end of the rec room, dodging the other fighting Alleys and mutants. They battled on the shredded remnants of the old Factory couch. As drips of Romeo's sweat splashed onto the mangled material, flashes of himself and his friends resting and playing on that very sofa inflamed the fire already inside him. He fought Bait as best he could, trying desperately to remember all he learned right there in Combat School, which seemed so very long ago.

Chapter Fifteen

Suddenly Max signaled his troops with a piercing whistle. As Romeo and Bait continued their duel on the floor, the rest of the Alleys slowly began to corner the mutants who were weak from exhaustion. Walking creepily on their hind legs, the Alleys backed every last creature to the edge of the room, trapping them like frightened children.

"What's gonna happen, mamma?" young Billy asked his mutated-dog mother.

"We'll be alright, son," she assured with hesitation, wrapping him tightly in her puffy arms. "We'll be just fine."

Sadly the Vent City dream of victory had ended. As the mutants huddled shaking and sobbing before the gruesome Alleys, their battered, disappointed faces dropped all the way to the floor. Even Romeo was ready to give up, his body giving out. He and Bait glared eye to eye, tangled together like a tight clamp, each waiting for the other's next move.

"Go ahead, *Stick*!" Bait slurred, his foul breath hovering like a black cloud. "Let's see what you gots!"

"Oh, yeah?" Romeo snapped back. "Whadaya think about this?" Romeo tweaked his right paw stabbing Bait in the shoulder. Shuddering from the sting, Bait's claws sunk menacingly into Romeo's side. This bloody bantering went on and on until suddenly out of nowhere…

Life Three

Fidel appeared at the creepy, old soup shaft near the back of the room in a puff of dusty air. Once a place where the soup pot elevator brought the happy-go-lucky Sticks to and from school, it now stood dark and empty much like Fidel himself. Slithering through the rec room, his beady, stabbing eyes sunk deep into their sockets glaring defiantly at his prey. His razor sharp claws tapped against the wooden floor like tiny needles across a chalkboard. He looked mad and deadly serious. A hush fell over the room as the impending terror sunk in. Not since that fateful nightmare five years earlier had the Vent City mutants seen the likes of Fidel. As he crept closer and closer to them, flashes of that toxic day rose to the surface of their suppressed memories, jolting their nerves. Just the sight of him and his cocky arrogance sent nasty visions of those large, horrible tanks spilling liquid death all over everyone, turning their lives into a hell on earth. In their minds they saw the horror again. The screaming faces and desperate escapes. The wicked grins slapped across every Alley. Fidel's demonic laugh echoing through the pipes, piercing their brains. And worst of all, remembering the cries, the endless bloodcurdling cries of helpless animals trapped under the poisonous, melting mess. The visions alone induced some of the mutants to vomit right there in front of the very devil himself who had began it all five years ago. For Romeo, seeing his archenemy so soon after their last encounter lit boiling anger deep within his chest. Knowing his father was being held by Fidel somewhere against his will, maybe having already been tortured or worse, filled his heart with rage. Still attached to Bait, the venom bubbling inside him erupted. "What are you trying to do, Fidel!" he shouted, surprised by his own audacity. "What are you doing here in our school?"

"What am I doing here? What am I doing here?" Fidel gnarled, twiddling his evil little bug jar and jangling his stolen ID tags. "I think the question is, what are you doing here?" He flexed his claws and slashed his paw through the air, causing each mutant to wince further and further into the tight corner. Standing like a dictator in front of the crowd, Fidel's eerie silent five loomed in the shadows. "You've got it all wrong, little Romeo. I don't know what stunt you and these *freaks* think you are trying to pull," he continued, his teeth clenched together, his body crouched low to the floor, "but did you think you could actually fight me and my army?" Fidel stared down at the mutants. "Who do you think you are? Tough guys? I don't know why you decided to show your grotesque faces in the first place, though I can *assume* Romeo has something to do with it," he stabbed in Romeo's direction. "But how *stupid* can you actually be? Don't you know nobody wants to look at you ever again? You're disgusting!"

Sizzling in the corner, the grieving mutants listened in shame.

"A long time ago I put you in your place," Fidel continued, "where you belong! You make me sick! I'm going to do this city a favor and finish the job I started before. I'm going to rip you all to pieces myself and then I'm going to..."

Suddenly a loud rumble bubbled beneath the floor, rocking and rattling the Factory like thunder. Scores of vengeful Sticks came bursting through the doors and windows, revenge burning in their eyes. Swarming the Factory like crazed bees, they tore through the room. Everyone was there, Waffles, Vittles, Soot, Ms. Purrpurr, Tabitha and Snickers, and even the three new guys. And at the front of the pack, good, old Calvin led the way leaving behind his moment in the spotlight to ride with those who needed him most. He passed Romeo with a wink, spinning excitement into the air. Immediately, Romeo's tangled insides felt the warm tingle of hope. Leaving Fidel quivering at his perch, Romeo ripped himself free from Bait and dashed through the rec room to join his friends. Seeing Romeo's excitement, the Vent City mutants felt revived. Leaping up from their misery, they charged into glory. Fluffy and Darla ran in mad circles around the stunned Alleys, keeping a watchful eye on Fidel who fumed ferociously in the center of the room.

"Get them, Alleys!" Fidel wailed. "Get them!"

Fidel's lot scurried through the room

slashing anyone and anything in their way. Now heavily outnumbered, the Alleys growled and shrieked desperately trying to maintain their brutal authority.

"Attack mode!" Vittles roared at the front of the room, his muscles pulsing. "Attack! Attack!"

Like vultures, the hungry Sticks swarmed the Alleys, gnawing and clawing at them with their well-groomed nails. Overcoming the shock of seeing the Vent City creatures for the very first time, they put aside their nausea and fright and fought side by side them like beasts themselves.

"Let me go! Let me go!" Steak wailed as Darla dragged him around by his wimpy tail. "Help! Help!"

"You wouldn't dare help me! Why should I help you?" she yelled with vengeance, viciously yanking two handfuls of fur right off his bottom. She tossed his hair in the air like snow.

On the other side of the room, smelly old Cheeseburger was tangled in a Tuesday and Murphy sandwich. Tugging on either side, they pulled him back and forth by his arms, flopping him from side to side like a clown.

"Stop it! You're hurting me!" he cried, slashing each of them in the face with his back paws.

"Oh shut up, fat boy!" Tuesday snapped, dodging out of the way of his beefy, orange claws.

"Nobody calls me fat boy!" Cheeseburger

howled managing to free his left paw, Tuesday still yanking on his right. With a roar, he grabbed Tuesday's little body and threw her flat against the floor. Standing as high as he could on his hind legs, he crashed down flattening her beneath him. Frantically, she wiggled and squirmed under his meaty belly. For his final clincher, Cheeseburger pressed himself firmly into the ground, savoring the mad cries and moans spitting from Tuesday's tortured mouth. "Take that, you stupid kitty!" he cackled, positioning his hefty bottom directly over her face.

"Nooo!" she screamed, his large rump slamming down against her.

Just then, Cheeseburger felt a piercing sting on his Alley back. Looking behind him, he saw sad little Murphy, half his size, feasting on the flab of his back. He dug his tiny, inexperienced claws into his thick flesh like a bug.

"Ouch!" Cheeseburger yelped, leaping off Tuesday. He danced wildly around trying to whip off Murphy.

Maximizing her advantage, Tuesday lunged at Cheeseburger, sinking her sharp teeth right into his leg.

"Ouch!" Cheeseburger yelled again, flopping onto the floor like a speared fish.

As the monstrous battles continued all around the room, Snickers found himself fighting off not one, but two grisly Alleys. In a deadly headlock, both Bait and Fink twisted his big, fat head back and forth, to and fro.

"Hee-hee-hee!" Bait giggled, biting at Snickers' ears.

"What a load o' fun! This is da' most fun I've had in a long time!" Fink laughed. "Bait, let *me* bite his ears for a while!"

"Be my guest," Bait mumbled with a mouthful of earwax.

Snickers was helpless to the two grungy Alleys. Whining and crying, he rolled around on the floor like Humpty Dumpty after the great fall. But then, just as Bait was about to finish Snickers off, Bradley and Hayward came bouncing out of nowhere. They savagely pecked at Bait and Fink with their tiny pigeon beaks and squirrel teeth, forcing them off poor, defenseless Snickers.

"It's another one of dem freaks!" Fink howled over Bradley's shoulder.

But Bait and Fink were soon getting the beating of their lives, trampled by weirdoes. It was a ghastly scene. Doomed and outnumbered, the Alleys hissed hard enough to knock their teeth out, but it was no use. They were losing. The fiery battle raged on as Bait and Fink pleaded like babies on the bloody, wooden floor.

The rec room war rampaged on like a football game gone awry. Almost comical in its outrageousness, the fur flew, blood gushed, and moans howled. Through all the mayhem, the few boneless animals shuffled on their little scooters, wheeling around like annoying, snotty children.

"Get outta here! What are you doing?" Delio hollered at one of the boneless as it wheeled right between him and another Alley. The squeaky wheels came to a full stop just as Delio was about to lunge forward. Yelling in mid-air, Delio landed instead on the boneless animal, knocking him off his wobbly scooter, freeing the Alley. The scooter took off with Delio on top.

"Thorry! Thorry!" the boneless yelled as his scooter picked up speed and crashed into the wall.

In spite of all the training, all the classes, all the preparation, the Sticks abandoned their earlier lessons and fought using their instincts. The Vent City mutants doing the same. The strong, street Alleys fought with a brutal immaturity to be reckoned with. Fidel thrived under the pressure, devilishly laughing, rubbing his evil paws together. Confident the Alleys would win in the end because they always did, Fidel spun around the room like a hurricane maintaining the level of chaos he so wickedly lived for.

"Keep fighting, my Alleys!" Fidel roared, savoring the sight of his enemies crumbling all around him. Then he spotted his ultimate conquest, Fidel's most delicious prey. Near the back of the room stood Romeo. Like a tiger, Fidel raced for him with his infamous, villainous hiss.

"Fidel! No!" Romeo screamed, desperately scurrying out of the way of the Alleys around him. But it was too late. Fidel pounced on him with such force, he knocked the wind right out of his lungs. "Let me go!" Romeo squealed, scampering on the floor. "Let me go!"

"Now I've got you right where I want you!" Fidel howled viciously in Romeo's ear, standing firmly on top of him.

"No!" Romeo cried and hissed desperately.

"Say your prayers, *domestick*! It's nighty-night for Romeo!" Fidel warned, holding his stabbing claws high above his head. His eyes swirled pure venom, sinisterly burning with the great spirits of the Alleys before him. Worst of all, that signature, demonic grin stretched across his face, sharp teeth hanging like icicles.

Terrified, Romeo shut his eyes tightly, when he suddenly heard his father's voice ringing out of the blue.

"Romeo! Romeo, I'm here!" the voice blared. "It's your father! I'm here, Romeo!"

A deadly silence fell over the battlefield as every animal froze. Simultaneously, they all saw Mr. Sox, Uncle Fred, and Mr. Gamble soar down the creaky, back stairs charging into the rec room to help. Following behind was none other than Fluffy, who had rescued them in the library before they could be killed.

"Your father?" Fidel wailed. "Your father? How could this Stick be your father? I *killed* your father! Have you forgotten that?"

Still bleached white, Mr. Gamble climbed up to the top of Fidel's crushed pillow palace and roared, "Romeo's right, Fidel! I'm back!"

Chapter Sixteen

Mr. Gamble's sudden appearance was just the slap in the face Fidel wasn't expecting. No one who remembered that long ago day could have ever expected him to return from the dead. Like a towering ghost, Gamble stood atop the pillows staring down every spiteful Alley with hatred in his eyes.

"I don't understand!" Fidel cried angrily. "You're dead! I killed you! Your rotten blood stained my paws! The smell of your death filled the street!"

"I remember," Mr. Gamble snarled, "but I had one life left! You counted wrong, Fidel!"

"That's impossible!" Fidel screamed. "You were dead for the ninth time! I waited for you to wake up, but you never did!"

"Oh, yes I did! And what did I wake up to? My dead wife!" Mr. Gamble swallowed the concealed lump in his throat, fighting the burning urge to slaughter Fidel at that second. "You killed her, Fidel! You killed my family too! Well, you *didn't* kill me, did you? And you *didn't* kill one of my sons!" Mr. Gamble stared wrathfully at Fidel. "Now we're *going* to kill you and save the feline society from your evil grasp! That you can be sure of!"

"Yeah, right!" Fidel cracked. "Jailbird!" he motioned, seeing the little black and white paws hiding in the corner. "Get him!"

"No, Fidel, I can't!" Jailbird whined as his fear intensified. He dropped to his knees in a groveling mess, his body quivering from a need for his growing dependency on the nip.

"I said get him! Do it now, you pathetic coward or they'll be no more nip for you!"

Like the king of the jungle himself, Mr. Gamble roared off the pillows. In slow motion, Fidel whipped around, his teeth bared for war. Mr. Gamble came tumbling down on top of him, but Fidel managed to flip him upside down, pulling villainously at his ears.

"I've got you now, and this time I know you're a niner!" Fidel hissed fiendishly. "Nobody makes a fool out of me!" Just as Fidel was about to kill Mr. Gamble for good, Romeo slammed into him like a home run baseball. "Ahhh!" Fidel shouted, tumbling face forward onto the hard ground. With his steel, ruby eyes, Fidel glared at Mr. Gamble, then lunged forward. As he did ten hideous dogs came pounding through the dreaded basement door, flying around the room like a tornado. They masked their shock at seeing the grisly mutants with looks of intense anger. Fidel flew back, falling flat on his bottom. At the head of the pack, little pug-nosed Bull sprayed gobs of gooey spit all over the place. Immediately behind him, his faithful lot growled savagely at the cats. Young Pierre stood proud and tall at the back.

"Where's my Basset?" Bull cracked enraged. "I said, where's my dog?"

"I...I...I, uh..," Fidel crawled backwards.

With devilish delight Bull roared, "Take him, boys! Drag him away with the rest of these worthless Alleys. We'll have to get the rest of the *lowlifes* another time!" He pointed at the shivering heap in the corner.

"Wait just a minute, Bull," Fidel pleaded with a phony smile. "Let's talk about this. I mean...what if we just..."

"Blah, blah, blah! *Now*!" Bull howled in the air. "Take him down, boys!"

Suddenly the dogs shot across the room knocking Romeo out of the way, barking and snapping through the fearful crowd. Fidel's retreating Alleys charged out the front entrance, stumbling over the dead mutants that lay defeated on the sidewalk. Then, several of the larger dogs encircled Fidel, howling and growling like wolves. Fidel flew between their strong legs and dashed for the door. The dogs followed closely behind him, barking their way down the tarred, city streets and off into nowhere.

It had finally happened. Fidel and the Alleys were gone.

For a long moment, a deadly silence hung over the rec room. Nobody moved an inch. Nobody made a sound. Outside, the wind whistled through the tiny cracks and crevices of the splintered Factory walls.

"Romeo, are you alright?" Mr. Gamble called out from atop of what was left of the pillows.

"Yeah, I'm over here, dad!" Romeo yelled back, wiggling out from under several torn books.

Running to each other like lovesick characters in a movie, they embraced, their back paws stuck to the floor in the slick reminders of war. With glossy expressions, the two held each other tightly as their bodies swayed back and forth.

"Yeah!" the crowd erupted, jumping high into the air.

"We did it! We did it!" the Sticks chanted. "We finally did it!"

"Ro-meo! Ro-meo! Ro-meo!" the Vent City-ites howled. Even Fluffy joined in the victory song. "Ro-meo! Ro-meo!"

Still in his father's arms, Romeo blushed feeling euphoric and appreciated. One thought however burned in his mind. "Don't thank me! Thank my father! Heck, thank yourselves! We all did it together!"

"Hurray!" they cheered again.

Near the door, Waffles had watched as the dogs chased Fidel and his gang clear out of sight. "They're gone! They're really gone!" he confirmed, rushing back to the celebration.

All at once, the Sticks and Vent City mutants grabbed hold of Romeo and Mr. Gamble. They lifted them high above their heads like winning trophies. In one massive huddle, they paraded their heroes around the messy room, tossing them up and down and calling out their names.

After the festivities died down, a much-anticipated reunion began. Emotions flying, Romeo, Fluffy, Tabitha, and Calvin had hardly seen the others since before their dreaded stay on the island. Tears started pouring as they each ran from one friend to the other.

"Listen up, everybody," Romeo said joyfully. "It's so good to be back at the Factory with all my friends."

"Romeo, I can't believe it's really you! I thought I'd never see you again!" cried Ms. Purrpurr. "Thank you for what you have done."

"I'd do it again, Ms. Purrpurr." Romeo smiled. He turned to Calvin. "Calvin buddy, you came through for us!"

"Yeah, well, even us stars need a break from all those cameras and reporters," he said shyly, nudging Romeo in the shoulder.

"Waffles! Vittles!" Fluffy shouted, running to hug them.

Snickers and Uncle Fred immediately ran up to Romeo as soon as they got the chance. "Hey, Romeo! I sure do wanna thank you for helping us," Snickers began, his eyes wandering all around. "I mean, it was pretty awful being stuck in that library all that time. I mean, I don't even like to read and there we were in the library and..."

"Uh...you're welcome, Snickers," Romeo interrupted. "It's great to see you again, too, but really you don't need to thank me. If you hadn't shown up when you did, who knows what the Alleys would have done."

Throughout the tearful reunion, Romeo searched for the one cat he longed to see the most. After a few minutes, he spotted Mr. Sox standing alone. Romeo didn't waste a second. With tears in his eyes, he crashed against him like a child.

"There, there, my young Romeo," Mr. Sox gently whispered in his ear. "My Romeo. I know, I know," he repeated over and over as Romeo wept softly in his arms. "You've been through so much for such a little one. Far too much. But you've done well, Romeo. You're a brave male, and I'm very proud of you."

Chapter Sixteen

"You...you are? Really?" Romeo said looking up.

"Yes," Mr. Sox nodded, lifting up his glasses. "And do you know what else?"

"What, Mr. Sox? What is it?" Romeo asked.

"Queen Elizabeth is proud of you too. I feel it," he said passionately.

With a heavy sigh, Romeo broke down again at those warm, yet painful words. Queen Elizabeth. It was all for her. Everything he did, it was all for her.

"Now tell me son, have you heard from dear Mr. Shadow since he escaped?" Mr. Sox inquired.

"No. I didn't even know that much," Romeo answered. "In fact, considering his legs, I didn't know what to think."

"Well, it's true, he escaped even before the others. And I think I have an idea who may have helped him," Mr. Sox said looking across the room. Sure enough, he found Twinkle Toes sitting alone in the corner.

"Beware of him, Mr. Sox," Romeo warned. "He's not who he used to be. He's one of *them* now. They call him Jailbird."

"Maybe not," Mr. Sox replied as he walked toward Twinkle Toes. With Romeo by his side, Mr. Sox peered down at the striking black cat. "Twinkle Toes? Is that you?"

With a nod, Twinkle Toes cracked a tiny smile.

"Wow!" Romeo beamed. "Is it really you? Are

you really back? Is it true?"

"Just simmer, dude!" Twinkle Toes said with a laugh.

"Tell me all about it! Did Fidel hurt you?" Romeo cried. "Does he know what you did for Mr. Shadow? You did save Mr. Shadow, right?"

Taking in a deep breath, Twinkle Toes wiggled his bottom closer to Romeo. "Right. Listen, I'm so sorry they made me do all those awful things! They made me do everything!" Clutching at his chest, he whined, "It was the nip! They put me on the nip, man! The nip....the nip.....It makes you lose your mind," he confessed as tiny beads of sweat formed on his brow. "Mr. Shadow, he's okay now. I think he's with his people or something. It was the least I could do."

Twinkle Toes went on to explain how Fidel had an evil hold on him, and when he began to sober up Fidel would feed him more nip. He described how he managed to sneak Mr. Shadow out late one night and smuggle in a big can of mace.

"Oh, my!" Romeo cried. "You did that too?"

As Twinkle Toes talked about his ordeal, Romeo noticed his body twitching and quivering, the obvious sobering effects of coming down from the nip again.

A little later on, Romeo introduced his heroic father and the Vent City mutants to his Factory friends. In time, the Sticks would hear all their shocking stories. A bit leery about how his friends would react to such oddities, he was delighted to see them embrace the others with compassion and love. Not surprising though, it was in the nature of a Stick.

Soon exciting plans had begun for the much-anticipated reconstruction of the Factory. First of all, the place needed a good cleaning. It was covered in rubbish and garbage. Once that was finished, the books needed rebinding, the chairs, couches, and pillows restuffed, and of course the faithful soup pot and elevator had to be completely repaired.

"Let's build a new and better litteroom! Bigger and deeper than before!" Darla shouted out, but no one paid any attention.

A low murmur hovered over the crowd.

"Mr. Sox, when do we get started?" Delio asked playfully attacking Tuesday's tail. She had to swat five times before he finally stopped.

"Yeah, Mr. Sox! What can I do?" Tabitha called out. "I want to help right away!"

"Me too, Mr. Sox!" shouted Uncle Fred. "I won't screw up this time, I promise!"

"What about me, Mr. Sox?" somebody else yelled.

"And me?" asked another.

"And me?"

"And me?"

Eager to get started, Mr. Sox calmed the

anxious group with a simple wave of his paw. "Slow down, children. Slow down. I think before we go any further, somebody *else* should be joining me up here." With a most heartfelt grin, Mr. Sox looked down from his bent podium and stretched out his right paw to Romeo. Romeo gazed at Mr. Sox with tears in his eyes as everyone slowly began to clap in unison.

"Go, go, go, go!" they chanted louder and louder. Mr. Gamble pushed Romeo to the front. Modestly, he moved through the wave of Sticks and mutants, grabbing Mr. Sox's awaiting paw as the older cat welcomed their new, young leader.

Stepping up to the podium, Romeo and Mr. Sox banded together, holding their inside paws high over their heads in victory. It was a grand moment for all.

"Speech! Speech! Speech!" the crowd cheered. Mr. Sox stepped back.

Hesitantly, Romeo quieted them. "My fellow friends, Sticks and Vent City dwellers alike, victory was ours today!" he shouted with a new found strength in his voice. "We've got our home back, and it's time to start our lives over again!"

"Yeah!" they cheered.

Facing the mutants he said, "Vent City is no longer your home! You are all welcome here at the Factory, faraway from the evil rats and dark forces that still plague the vents! We are all one now!"

Chapter Sixteen

"Hurray!"

"But our fight is not over," Romeo continued. "We may have our beloved Factory back, but the city is still full of Alleys just waiting for their revenge! We must...we must..." Suddenly, sweat poured from Romeo's forehead as he grabbed his belly and toppled to the floor. The crowd gasped. Mr. Gamble raced to him.

"He fainted! Romeo fainted!" Mr. Gamble cried, fanning Romeo's face.

Because of her excellent work helping Mr. Shadow with his broken legs, Tabitha was immediately summoned. "He's burning up," she said feeling Romeo's clammy nose. "He needs a doctor right away!"

"He's been really sick all week," Mr. Gamble explained. "Fluffy and I were able to snatch him some antibiotics from the Vet, but they're all gone now. This fight today was too much for him in his condition! Oh no! What's going to happen to my son?"

Just then Romeo mumbled, his eyelids flickering. "Wha...what happened? Where am I?"

Mr. Sox looked down at him with marked worry. "My boy, you fainted. We've got to get you home."

Weak and weary, Romeo could barely stand. Looking worse than before, he had new bumps and bruises on top of the old ones. His fever was soaring and his vision blurry. During the day's battles, he was fueled by passion and rage, but now that it was over he was crashing hard. Any fleeting ounce of energy he mustered had been completely whipped out of him.

While a quiet vigil took place at the Factory for mutants dead in action, Romeo headed home with his father and good friend, Tabitha. On the way they kept a tight grip on their sick, little hero. Because of the dogs' attack on the Alleys, the three didn't worry much about their return. They were safe for a while.

"Lean against me, Romeo," Mr. Gamble said as they trudged through the cold city. "Don't worry about falling. I've got you."

"Sorry I haven't been around much, Romeo," Tabitha said softly. "I've just been too scared to leave. I never want to be away from home like that again," she admitted.

"Don't worry about it, Tab. You came out and helped us today when we needed it most. That's the important thing," Romeo said with a phlegmy cough.

"Gosh, you sure sound bad," Tabitha flinched. "Mr. Gamble, is he going to be alright? All that gurgling can't be good, can it?"

Mr. Gamble kept one shoulder pressed against Romeo's body, propping him up like an old drunk. "Of course he's going to be alright. Dennis will take care of him once he gets home. Besides, nothing can stop my boy. He's number one!" Proudly, Mr. Gamble patted Romeo's back with his tail.

"Awe quit it, dad, I'm nothing special," Romeo cooed weakly.

"Nothing special? Nothing special?" Mr. Gamble said, his eyes scrunched together. "Are you kidding?" He paused on the cracked sidewalk and stared Romeo in the face. "You are something *very* special. Who saved this whole day? Who stood up to Fidel? And not for the first time, I might add? Who fought fiercer than the best warriors in the history of time? Who....?"

"Alright! Alright, dad! I believe you! I believe you!" Romeo blushed, smiling coyly at the ground, twisting his back paw in nervous circles.

"Ro-meo! Ro-meo!" Tabitha chanted, dancing playfully around him.

"Did you see the look on Fidel's face when those hounds came charging in?" Mr. Gamble asked with a laugh.

"I've never seen him look so funny! I didn't know a jaw could fall that close to the floor," Tabitha giggled.

"I guess you're right," Romeo chuckled with a sudden burst of energy. "And when Bull asked about that Basset? I wish I had a photo of Bait when he heard that one!"

"Great idea! Imagine if we could sell it! We'd

make millions!" Mr. Gamble roared, breaking into uncontrollable laughter. "I can see it now, *Get your photos of Fidel and Bait crying like babies! Only three salmon each!* Ha! That'd be great! Every Stick would want one!"

Pretty soon, all three of them were bouncing home, laughing and cheering at the Alleys' expense. In fact, they were having such a good time, they almost forgot poor Romeo was sick. The more they laughed, the stronger he felt. And boy, did they laugh.

"....and remember when you stuck your claws right into Bait's leg?" Tabitha wailed. "I saw that all the way across the room! I thought his eyes were going to pop out!"

"And what about that female, Tuesday? Did you see when that big, fat Alley tried to sit on her? I know she's not the nicest Stick, but man, I wouldn't want to be in her paws!" Romeo reminisced.

"And did you know that..," Mr. Gamble went on as the three of them carefully climbed up to Romeo's window. "...and then he threw up all over himself!"

"Gross, Mr. Gamble! Why'd you tell me that story?" Tabitha asked with her paw over her mouth.

"Oh, Tab, I've got stories that'll *really* gross you out!" Mr. Gamble exploded right as Romeo reached Dennis's open window. "Well Romeo, it's been a great day for all of us!" Mr. Gamble said giving Romeo a high-five. "We'll wait here until you're in safely."

"Come find me tomorrow," Tabitha said. "As long as you're feeling better, that is."

"I feel fine," Romeo answered back. "All this laughing did the trick! Besides, I've still got two more pills waiting for me inside."

Just before Romeo slipped in through the open window, he looked at his father and Tabitha and imitated the best, silliest Fidel face he could make.

"Stop it, Romeo! You're killing me!" Mr. Gamble howled, laughing so hard he nearly fell off the vine.

"You look just like him!" Tabitha wailed.

Still chuckling, Romeo leapt from the sill down to the familiar floor. Peeking behind him, he saw his father and Tabitha still outside. Feeling charged and alive, he stretched his back on Dennis's shaggy carpet and smiled. Just then, Pierre came sauntering in from the hallway. His posture was low and his nose pointed down.

"Hey, buddy!" Romeo yelled at him. "You really came through for us today. I owe you a big apology. I..."

"Romeo, you...you...," Pierre stuttered.

"What it is, Pierre?" Romeo asked. "Awe, come on. Whatever it is, tell me later. I'm in too good of a mood. I just want to eat and..."

"No, Romeo, you don't understand," Pierre whispered, a tear streaming down his furry face.

Suddenly, Romeo's massive grin faded and his heart started to pound. "What is it, Pierre? Is it about Fidel? Did something happen?" He began to pace around the rug. "Oh, no. Did he escape the dogs? Did he say something about me?"

"No, no. You don't understand. It's...it's..."

"Well, tell me! What happened?"

Just then, Dennis and his parents walked into the doorway. Pierre leaned against the doorframe and sunk to the floor.

"Oh, Romeo! You look awful," Dennis said with a shiver, grabbing Romeo in his arms. "I thought about you all day at school."

As Dennis cried, Romeo glanced over his shoulder. Pierre wouldn't even look at him. Mr. and Mrs. Crumb held onto each other dearly, looking very sad indeed.

"Gosh, Dennis," Mrs. Crumb began looking down at Romeo. "I hoped I wouldn't have to say this, but I think he looks much worse."

"Let us know if you need anything, Dennis," Mr. Crumb assured. "We're here for you." He walked out of the room, patting his son on the shoulder. "Don't forget, we go to the Vet's tomorrow morning at eight. And remember what he said, Romeo won't feel a thing. He'll just go right to sleep like he always does."

Chapter Sixteen

"It's for the best, honey," Mrs. Crumb said, her swelling nose getting redder.

"Sorry," Pierre mouthed, then he crawled under the bed.

What could they be talking about? Romeo wondered. *What about the Vet? I have a very bad feeling about this.*

Together, Romeo and Dennis sat in his room all evening just staring at each other for hours. In spite of sneaking his last two pills, Romeo's fever was rising again and his new battle wounds were beginning to settle in for a long stay. Eight A.M. was only one night's sleep away. Romeo knew something was up. But what? Of course Mr. Gamble had heard everything from the window ledge outside. Unfortunately, he knew exactly what was going to happen.

Chapter Seventeen

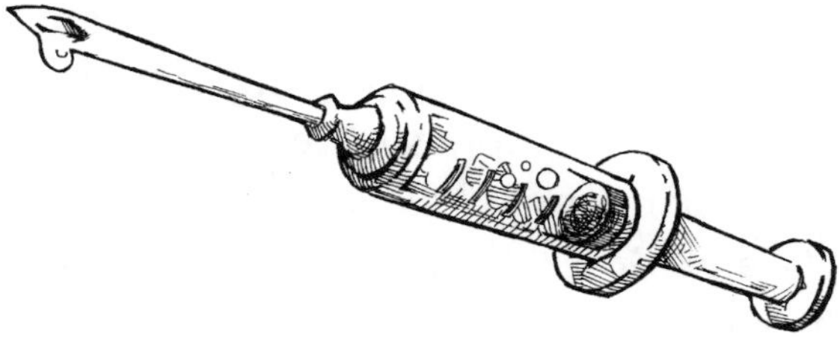

As Dennis ate his soggy hamburger and carrots, Romeo sat alone on the bed curled up underneath Dennis's pillow. The room was painfully quiet except for Mrs. Crumb's clinking dinner dishes in the kitchen and the occasional taxi horn outside. The cabbies gave up on their strike. They needed money. Pierre sat anxiously at attention, waiting for the moment to find just the right thing to say.

"Uh, Romeo? I'm real sorry about all zis," Pierre admitted very uncharacteristically. "I bet it is going to hurt."

Romeo didn't move. Pierre leapt onto the bed, staring deeply into the cowboy drawings on the pillowcase. "Are you okay?" he said as if to one of the cowboys, the seam cutting off his nose. "Romeo? What are you doing under there?"

"Go away," vibrated out of the horses and their silvery stirrups.

Inching his way closer, Pierre stuck his little, wet nose under the flap of the pillowcase. "Awe, come on. There's no sense in crying."

"I said go away!" Romeo exploded, shaking the pillow right onto the floor. "I know what's going on here! I figured it out! I'm getting the *Sleepy Potion,* aren't I?" Sleepy Potion was the phrase on the street for animals being put to sleep. SP for short.

"Calm down, Romeo! I know this is hard, but if it were *moi,* I'd be dead for good!" It didn't matter what Pierre said. Romeo was devastated. He was shivering and rubbing his itchy, red eyes. By now his new bumps had bloomed into full form and his fever had created a stinky, clammy film over his entire body. "I heard them talking about it when Dennis was at school, *oui*?" Pierre began, trying hard not to look at Romeo for too long. It was obvious he didn't want to be looked at. "They said you were just too sick to take care of. Zey don't want to do it, really! But *mon ami,* why don't you run away? Get out before morning?"

"I can't do that, Pierre. I can't even stand up. There's nothing I can do. Now why don't you just leave me alone?" Romeo whispered, a hollow stare on his sad face.

"But I..."

"Please, Pierre, I just want to be alone."

With a heavy sigh, Pierre nodded his head and jumped onto the floor. As he slugged his way through the valley of socks and crumpled homework, he paused a moment before leaving the room. Glancing up at Romeo on his deathbed, he grazed his paw slowly along the doorframe. "You were *tres* great today, Romeo. I was glad...I was glad to know you. To fight by your side."

With a slight smile, Romeo tilted his head up. "Thanks, Pierre. Thanks a lot."

Pierre slipped out of the somberness of the room with an unexpected pinch in his heart. While he lethargically dined on the uneaten portion of Dennis's soggy hamburger, Romeo stared at the stucco ceiling, a numbness slowly devouring his very soul.

Early the next morning, Dennis awoke to the shrieking sounds of his torpedo alarm clock, a gift from his loony Uncle Tom, a Navy man. Every morning it turned Dennis's messy room into an explosive warship. Once Uncle Tom came for a weekend visit and after hearing Dennis's alarm sound, he dove under the bed shouting out commands and holding his breath for dear life. Dennis threw his bear at the alarm. The sirens and explosions stopped.

Opening his crusty eyes, Dennis realized Romeo wasn't with him on the bed. He sat alone on Dennis's unkempt desk, staring blankly outside. Romeo could see Gwen's window across the Alley.

Chapter Seventeen

Her new pretty, pink shades were still closed.

"Dennis, are you awake?" Mrs. Crumb yelled from her hot bath. With the heating bill still not paid, she took full advantage of the hot water for as long as she could before it was shut off. "Honey? We'll have to go soon!"

"I'm up. I'm up," Dennis whined, still wrapped in all his blankets.

Lazily, Dennis slithered out of bed and began to get ready for the big day, all the while keeping a concerned eye on Romeo.

About thirty minutes later, Mrs. Crumb informed Dennis it was time to go. "You grab Romeo and meet me downstairs in five minutes," she hollered. "I'm going to see if I can get a cab."

"Whatever," Dennis mumbled, slipping on his mismatched socks.

After he was fully dressed, Dennis sat on his bed with his head in his hands. Slumped over, he cried and cried into his old teddy bear, his nose running all over the bear's ears. On the desk Romeo watched him sadly. For a cat like him, dying was simply a part of life. He'd be up and about in an hour or so after the execution, but Dennis didn't know that. Dennis couldn't know that. This would really be good-bye to Dennis, forever.

"Well Romeo, I guess this is it," Dennis sniffled onto his sleeve. "I can't believe this is happening. Maybe you could get better right now. Then maybe...."

"See you downstairs, Dennis," Mrs. Crumb cried from the hall.

Dennis dropped his head back into his hands. "I better get your box. I'll be right back."

Watching this gut-wrenching scene, Pierre sat still on the floor unsure of exactly what to do. "So...uh, you'll be back later tonight. I mean, you are a cat and you'll be alive, right?"

"Yeah, I'll be alive, but I won't be back here. Never," Romeo sighed.

"*Quoi*? What do you mean, never? I thought..."

"Once I die, I've died forever to Dennis. I can't ever let him see me again. That would be the ultimate sin. Bubastis would never forgive me."

"But, you've got to come back! Don't get me wrong, I'm not *that* crazy about you, but what will Dennis do? Did you see how sad he was?" Pierre asked nervously.

Romeo closed his eyes allowing a single tear to fall down his face. "That's just the way it is. There's nothing else I can do."

"Well, how are you going to get out of the Vet's office anyway? Once they kill you, do zey just leave you there, or what?" Pierre hounded.

Romeo hadn't thought about that. How *was* he going to get out of that office? "They'll probably send my dead body to the Pound to be chopped up into food for the inmates and eaten or something. I don't know, I don't care anymore anyway."

"Don't say that Romeo," Pierre said tenderly. "What do you mean you don't care, huh?"

Romeo leapt off the desk, crawled across the room and leaned his feverish body against the bedpost. "I don't know. What's the point if I can't be with Dennis? Just when I think I'm happy, something bad happens. I'm better off dying for good."

"You can't say zat! That's really bad. Don't say zat." Pierre cried. "I met your dad and I don't think he'd agree, *tu sait*?"

"Whatever. Look, I gotta go. Have a nice life," Romeo said flatly. "Maybe I'll see you one of these days. And oh, thanks again for your help yesterday."

For a long moment, Romeo and Pierre just sat there. Pierre not knowing what else to say and Romeo slipping farther and farther into his deep depression. He looked around the room woefully for the very last time, remembering all the happy moments he and Dennis shared together. All the times he fought hard just to find his way home. Standing there against the bedpost, Romeo thought of the very first day he arrived at the Crumbs'. It was a rainy day, a dreary day, but a special day. Dennis was so excited to find him when he came home from school. He said Romeo was the best birthday present in the whole wide world. For Romeo, he not only got a new family that long ago day, but he also got his name, Romeo Crumb. He loved Dennis and the Crumbs with all his heart. He knew this was not how any of them wanted things to end. Romeo slid off the desk and said his goodbyes. "Goodbye cowboy sheets," Romeo whispered, gently touching them with his paw. "Please keep Dennis warm." He stepped deeper into the room. "Goodbye ugly rug and smelly socks. Goodbye school books, water dish, mirror, toys and canned food. Goodbye magazines and beautiful, old desk." Eyes filled with tears, Romeo jumped on the desk one last time, staring out the window and into the room he still called Queen Elizabeth's. Through the sheer pink curtains, Romeo swore he saw Gwen herself cuddling Twinkle Toes. *He made it home, I knew he would,* Romeo said to himself. *Good for him.*

"Let's go, Romeo," Dennis said sadly re-entering the room. Holding the harsh cat carrier in his arms, he glanced down at Romeo's weak body. "Forget the box. I'll just hold you myself," he said warmly.

As Dennis picked Romeo up and walked toward the door, Romeo looked over at Pierre. "Goodbye," he mouthed as he bobbed in Dennis's arms. In an instant he and Dennis's room were forever gone from sight.

The big, yellow taxicab screeched into the morning traffic, splashing mud all over its rusting doors. From where he sat on Dennis's lap, Romeo wondered what would become of him. Would he ever see Dennis again? Would Dennis forget all about him once it was over? That could never be true. Romeo knew he wouldn't be forgotten.

At the Vet the familiar antiseptic smells, white uniforms, and swinging doors triggered bad memories nauseating Romeo and twisting his insides into knots. Mrs. Crumb checked them in. Dennis sat with Romeo on one of the orange waiting room chairs. Romeo sat curled in his lap as Dennis gently stroked his back. It hurt a little, but Romeo was far too weak to do anything about it. Besides, everything hurt. Dennis was crying, even in front of all the people in the waiting room.

All around him other nervous patients waited, sick animals who would soon be going home, home to fresh food and warm beds. Romeo knew he'd never go home again.

After ten torturous minutes, Romeo and Dennis were led through the swinging door with the circular window and placed into a small examining room. The medicine smells were stronger in that room than they had been in the other. So much in fact, that Romeo vomited all over Dennis's shoes. Mrs. Crumb waited patiently from her orange chair.

"Well, well, well, just who do we have here?" Dr. Stein asked, breezing into the tiny room. "Ah, Dennis Crumb." The doctor threw a metal clipboard on the counter and grabbed a small jar of purple goo. "I'll be back in a sec," he said slipping out once again.

"Doc, are you sure there's nothing you can..," Dennis called, the door slamming abruptly in his face. His mother followed the Vet into the hall. Dennis wheeled over the doctor's little chair and sat beside the examining table. "I'm sorry, Romeo. I really wish there was something else I could do," he began. "You see, if we could only get that medicine, you'd be okay. But, the doctor said even with that medicine you could still be sick for a really long time and dad said that would just cost too much money. And you'd suffer. I don't want to see you suffer. I'm sorry I let you down, buddy," he cried holding Romeo's front paws in his hand. "I guess it's my fault. I shouldn't have let you outside so much with all that rain and stuff."

Romeo tilted his head and stared into Dennis's glossy eyes. He so desperately wanted to tell him he was wrong. He was wonderful to him, absolutely wonderful.

"Dennis, can you come out here a minute?" his mother's voice rang from the hall. "Dennis?"

"I'm coming!" he yelled back, nuzzling his head into Romeo's belly. "I'll be right back, Romeo."

As he stepped out of the room, Dennis glanced tenderly at Romeo from the doorway and ran to his mother. Romeo lay helpless and alone on the cold, metal table.

Dennis had left the door open revealing all the cages of boarded or sick animals that lined the hallway. Immediately, Romeo noticed a familiar face in one of the lower cages. "Mr. Shadow!" he yelled with his last bit of strength. "It's me, Romeo! Mr. Shadow! Over here!"

Chapter Seventeen

"R-Romeo? Romeo? Is that really you?" Mr. Shadow searched with his eyes, clutching at the cage bars.

"It's me! It's really me!" Romeo called out. "But, I don't understand. What are you doing here? How are your legs? Shouldn't you be at home?"

A nurse suddenly walked by and Mr. Shadow flinched back to the rear of his cage. "It's my people," he said as soon as the woman passed. "They want me to stay here until my legs get better. Something about not wanting to deal with it." With his front paw, he rubbed his back legs. "To tell you the truth, I feel much better and it's not so bad here, you know. Anything's better than that hanging prison box at the Factory. *Anything*!"

"But, aren't you lonely here? Do they feed you?" Romeo poked.

"Really, it's not so bad. They feed me, and I talk to the other guys here when they're not sleeping, that is," he explained, pointing to three lazy looking cats in the cages beside him.

"Oh," Romeo sighed, dropping his tired head back to the table.

"But what about you? Why are you here?" Mr. Shadow asked.

Romeo started balling, tears streaming from his eyes.

"What is it, Romeo? What's wrong?"

"I'm...I'm getting SP'ed!"

"Oh, no! That's terrible!" Mr. Shadow mournfully stuck his nose between the bars. "I'm sorry, Romeo. I'm so sorry. You poor thing. You've lost so much already! At least it doesn't hurt. In fact, it's quite an easy death."

"It's not that. It's Dennis. He's so sad, and well, I'll never be able to see him again."

"Why, of course you will, you'll just..." Suddenly, it hit Mr. Shadow that Romeo was right. His life with Dennis would have to be over. He knew how much he loved Dennis. "Romeo, I wish I had the right thing to say. This is all the fault of those damn Alleys. I swear, I'm going to really get them back one day, you'll see."

Mr. Shadow watched Romeo wipe a tear rolling down his sad face. "Go find Fluffy or one of the others. They'll look after you until we get the Factory back," the old teacher said.

"We got it back. Yesterday. I was so happy then, but now I just don't know how to feel."

"The Factory is back? That's great!" Mr. Shadow glowed, sitting up tall. "All you have to do is go back to the Factory and..."

Just then, Dennis returned with Dr. Stein. Mr. Shadow caught one last glimpse of Romeo as the examining room door slammed shut.

"Alright, Dennis, let's take this little guy into the...*other* room," the doctor motioned, checking his reflection in the x-ray machine.

Chapter Seventeen

As Dennis scooped up his dear cat, Romeo let out a dismal meow and allowed himself to be carried into the *other* room. There he was again placed on a cold, metal table, this one larger than the last and situated next to a small tray covered in ghastly looking needles. The rest of the room was filled with more metal tables, more trays of needles, and other gruesome, pointy objects. All sorts of weird contraptions sat over in the corner and one dangling light hovered over his head. Jars and bottles of putrid looking liquids lined the counters, and about five or so nurses scurried around the room looking busy. "The first thing you should know, Dennis, is that it'll take only a few seconds for Romeo to...fall asleep," Dr. Stein explained, winking at one of the blond nurses. "He'll get sleepy first and then...well, it's very peaceful."

Dennis listened intently to the doctor's words as he pet Romeo's clammy backside. Romeo was too tired to listen, but he did suddenly hear another sound coming from behind Dr. Stein. Above his head was a small window. Outside that window clinging to a heavy branch was none other than his father, Mr. Gamble. "What? What are you doing?" Romeo mouthed in shock, keeping one eye on Dennis and the doctor.

With his right paw, Mr. Gamble waved across the window, presumably signaling something to Romeo.

"Huh?" Romeo said with his eyes, his heart beating faster.

Shaking his wet head, Mr. Gamble jolted back

and forth on the branch, trying desperately to communicate something.

What are you doing? Romeo wondered.

"...and then Candy here will take his body in the back to be...," the doctor drummed on to Dennis's nodding head.

"Don't worry!" Mr. Gamble mouthed as clear as he could behind the foggy glass.

Romeo squinted his eyes together and shook his weary head.

"Don't worry!" Mr. Gamble mouthed again slower.

Suddenly, Romeo felt the doctor's cold hands reaching around his neck. "Here Dennis, you'll probably want to keep this." He handed Dennis Romeo's collar.

In the window, Mr. Gamble's eyes widened like two satellite dishes, his jaw dropping like an anchor. "No! No! No!" he screamed, waving his paws back and forth. "You'll need that!"

"Okay Dennis, it's time." Dr. Stein reached for one of the longer needles and filled the syringe with a clear liquid. With his left arm, he gently held Romeo's little head and began to lower the needle toward his body.

"Wait!" Dennis screamed. "Isn't there anything else we can do? Anything at all? Please! There's got to be something you can do?" he begged desperately.

Chapter Seventeen

"I'm sorry, Dennis, but there's really nothing else we can do to keep Romeo from suffering. Believe me, I know how hard this is." Adjusting the swinging light above him, he again proceeded to lower the needle. "It's the most humane thing for Romeo. He'd thank you if he could."

Dennis flung himself against Romeo's body. "I'm sorry, Romeo!" he cried as the needle pierced into Romeo's leg. "I love you! I'll love you forever and ever and ever! I'll never forget you! Don't go, Romeo! Please don't go!"

As the serum raced through his veins, Romeo could hold back no longer. He cried with Dennis, moaning and groaning as the liquid swirled further into his body.

"I'd like to be alone with my cat," Dennis wept.

The doctor nodded and left with the nurses. Mr. Gamble watched from the window as Romeo became more and more drowsy, his breathing becoming slower and choppy. When Romeo finally closed his eyes, Dennis let out a scream and collapsed on the table holding Romeo in his arms. "Don't go! Don't go!" he pleaded. "Romeo! Don't leave me!"

With Romeo's precious collar clutched in his hand, Dennis took one last look at his dying cat. "Maybe it's true what they say about cats. Maybe, just maybe, you do have nine lives." With tears in his eyes, he ran out of the room and back into his

Life Three

mother's arms. "I can't take it anymore!" he yelled. "I can't watch him die! I just can't!"

"That's okay, son," Mrs. Crumb said warmly, gently stroking Dennis's head, her own heart broken as well.

Mrs. Crumb paid the small fee and together she and her grieving son left for home. In the *other* room, Romeo lay alone and scared on the table, barely breathing. With little time to spare, Mr. Gamble pried open the small window and ran to his side. Death was death, even if only temporary. He cupped Romeo in his arms and rocked him gently. "Romeo, your mother was the most beautiful creature I'd ever seen. Her eyes were like moonbeams, really, and her hair as soft as cotton. Her laugh, oh Romeo, her laugh..."

Romeo laid his head down and whispered, "I love you too, Dennis," before taking his final breath and dying in his father's arms.

"...you've got her smile," Mr. Gamble went on, still rocking Romeo on his lap.

Chapter Eighteen

As Romeo lay there dead, Mr. Gamble wept, gently stoking his son's tail and tweaking his ears. But he found himself a bit sick in the stomach, for even though Romeo would soon be awake, the sight of a dead cat was always hard to swallow, especially when it's your son. Suddenly, Mr. Gamble heard the doctors and nurses talking outside and knew time was of the essence. Putting his paw to his lips, he sounded a loud, piercing whistle. In a flash, Calvin and Snickers appeared at the tiny window. "We've got to do it now! The nurses are coming for him!"

Snickers and Calvin pushed themselves around in the open crack of the window. "Hurry up! Get in there!" Calvin snapped, shoving Snickers' huge behind through the opening.

"Quit it! I'm moving as fast as I can!" Snickers

barked, his belly fat oozing over the windowsill.

"Will you two cut it out and get in here? The nurse will be back any second!"

Snickers and Calvin finally fell into the room. Once inside, they hopped up on the table next to Mr. Gamble. "Boy, he's really dead, ain't he?" Snickers said morbidly.

"Yes, yes, he is. Now, you grab his shoulders and I'll get his back," Mr. Gamble said in a hurry, hearing the sound of squeaky, white shoes approaching. "Hurry up! No goofing around!"

"Yeah, Calvin! No goofin' around!" Snickers warned, lifting Romeo's back legs. "You know, the last time I was at the Vet, I had to get this really long bath. It was terrible. All that soap got in my eyes, and they stuck this thing in my ear. Oh! And then they lifted my tail and..."

"Oh, shut up and move!" Mr. Gamble hollered, his temper quickly rising. "I wish we had that collar!" he moaned, peeking on the floor to see if Dennis dropped it in his distraught state.

Romeo was finally carried over to the window and lifted onto the branch outside. "Be very careful!" Mr. Gamble shouted to the others seeing them nearly drop him three stories down. "If you cause him to lose more than one life, I swear, you'll be sorry!"

"What's the difference? He's dead anyway!" Calvin cried, half in the room, half on the branch.

"Just be careful!" Mr. Gamble shouted again.

With Snickers, Calvin, and Romeo safely on the tree branch, Mr. Gamble hurried himself out of the room and closed the window shut. "I see the door opening! They're coming! They're coming!"

Two nurses promptly walked into the room, spotting the empty table.

"Where'd he go?" one asked the other.

"I don't know! Did the boy take him?"

"No, I saw him leave with his mother. What'll we tell Dr. Stein?"

"Oh, just tell him we took care of it. I just wanna get out of here. You know, coffee break."

"I hear ya," the nurse agreed. Leaving their nurses' hats on the counter, they took one more quick glance around the room and left without another word.

On the tree, Mr. Gamble and the others carefully carried Romeo down to the ground.

"Where's his collar?" Calvin asked.

"The Vet gave it to Dennis, so be extra alert," Mr. Gamble warned.

"Got it!"

After a long, rainy walk, the cats finally made it all the way to the Factory carrying Romeo's body like an ant does with his faithful friend's corpse. They hid as best they could from the early morning walkers.

At the Factory several of Romeo's friends had been awaiting his arrival, eager to talk to him about the exciting recent events. Some of the older ones like

Mr. Sox stayed home with their families, unwilling to come back just yet. The rest knew of Mr. Gamble's plan and came without hesitation. Sitting on the icky floor, they gathered in a circle sharing their hopes and dreams for the future. While their lives were getting back on track, the Factory itself was a total disaster area and needed immediate scrubbing. The leftover Alley smells alone were difficult enough to endure. Darla and Waffles had already begun mopping up the floor, and some of the others were cleaning as well. When Mr. Gamble arrived, Romeo's lifeless body was placed on one of the few remaining pillows. Of course Fidel's pillows were thrown out back. Who'd want to lay on those?

After an hour or so, it finally happened. Romeo's scars disappeared like magic and he began to come to. "Wh..wh..where am I? Wh..what hap.. pened?" Romeo quivered with his old stutter. "Momma?" he whispered, lifting up his head.

"No, no, Romeo, you're at the Factory, remember?" Mr. Gamble said with a smile of relief. "You're back with us. We're here to take care of you."

Looking at all his blurry friends, Romeo grabbed his father's paw. "She reached out to m..me this time, fath..ther. Sh..she did."

"What? What Romeo?" Mr. Gamble asked. "Look, get some rest. Everyone will be here for a while."

"N..no dad, she tried to touch m..me," Romeo said slowly.

Mr. Gamble moved closer. "Who, Romeo? Who are you talking about? Who reached out to you."

"Mom did. Sh..sh..she comes to m..me every time I die. Th..this time she a..almost touched me. But she didn't look at me. She didn't look."

Just then, Romeo noticed Candle. She was staring at him from the corner of the room, hidden in the dark shadows. She looked sweet and fragile, like a little lost girl. "What's sh..she doing here?" Romeo asked softly.

Candle lowered her head and closed her eyes. A look of shame and embarrassment covered her face. She seemed tired and frightened and alone.

"Never mind her," Mr. Gamble insisted. "She was released late last night. Forget about her, she needs to leave anyway. Back to your mother, what were you saying?"

While Mr. Gamble's voice droned on, Romeo caught a tiny sparkle reflecting off Candle's tears. For one brief moment their eyes locked. It was as if for that second everything was quiet and still. In his mind she was an Alley, however kinder and gentler than most, yet he noticed something different about her but he didn't know what it was.

"D..Dennis. I miss Dennis," Romeo cried deliriously, snapping out of the trance Candle had him in.

"I know. I know, son. Now, about your mother? Think hard," Mr. Gamble prodded.

Suddenly, Soot and Vittles came bursting through the rec room door crashing hard to the ground from exhaustion.

"Where have you two been?" Waffles asked throwing down his makeshift mop. "Vittles, who's guarding the front door?"

"We've got news! News about Fidel!" Soot exploded between breaths.

"What is it? Is he coming this way?" Mr. Gamble roared with anger. "Oh, no! Is he with the other Alleys?"

"No, nothing like that," Soot continued.

"Then what is it?" Mr. Gamble demanded.

Vittles and Soot looked at each other and then around the room. After a long pause, Waffles stepped forward. "It's Fidel, sir. He's dead...for good. Some Alleys just told me."

With a sudden gasp, Romeo's eyes rolled back into his head and he passed out cold. Mr. Gamble did the same.

The next two years would be filled with some of the best, most happy days of the Sticks' lives. Except for Romeo. His life would never be the same.